Sideout for Murder

43,400 words

by Paula Murphy

Sideout for Murder © 2008 by zanybooks.com

Cover photo by Samuel Knochs III

ISBN 978-0-9841603-1-0

This book is a work of fiction and any resemblances to persons, living or dead, places, events, or locales is purely coincidental. They are productions of the author's imagination and used fictitiously.

To obtain permissions, write *support@zanybooks.com*

To purchase more fine books like the one you're reading, go to *http://zanybooks.com.*

Chapter 1

There's nothing better than a sunny day at the beach—at least, once one finds a place to park. A clear blue-sky overhead, a long line of foaming white breakers in a blue green sea, even the occasional flash of silver as a fish breaks the water. Add a bikini-clad crowd of sun worshipers working on their tans, a glimpse of sails on the horizon, and it is as close to perfection as a day can be.

Then why was I sitting with my back to the waves watching game after game of beach volleyball?

Two reasons. First, I was a guest at the Lackland Beer Women's Beach Championships, a guest of that very special person in my life. Second, it was one of the few and only times that person has lent full approval to my watching bikini-clad blonds cavorting in the sand.

Say what you will about women athletes in other sports, in volleyball the athletes are as curved or curvier than the girl next door. Flat tennis-player bellies, lean flanks, and long lean legs that reached the limits of my imagination.

Take the lithesome twins that I'd watched as they progressed up the rungs in the early rounds of the tournament. Twin blond pony tails, twin wet-look bikinis in a shocking pink, twin dimpled bellies in a golden tan, and twin bikini tops that held their own small secrets high above the sand. Add to this a talent that could send the two leaping six feet in the air and keep them hanging above the net for what seemed hours to their terrorized opponents, and you had a team of two sure tournament winners.

Alas, a somewhat muscular brunette and her slim blond companion eliminated the twins in the quarterfinals, rather decisively in fact. But on second appraisal, the brunette wasn't that muscular and her blue one-piece revealed a rather generous amount of curve. The slim blond companion was only slim in the leg; her gray bikini top held more than the twins had between them, and to watch her body soar into the air was to watch an R-rated film played in slow motion.

I was not alone in my admiration. Courtside was crowded with bronzed bodies, surfers, several generations of volleyball professionals and volleyball players to be, mothers and fathers just past the age of playing this grueling sport, a couple of hundred children who didn't seem to belong to anyone in particular, and a camera crew from a local cable network (the only ones who ever seem to cover volleyball). The tournament organizers had outdone themselves.

Our vantage point was a blanket an ideal three feet from courtside (we were roughing it; most spectators had a comfortable beach chair at the very least). Marlene, that very special person in my life, kept cutting me slices of cold fresh melon along with thin slices of ham. Add wedges of Jarlsberg cheese, a dash of lime, and sips of the white wine we had concealed in a water bottle and, yes, you could still say my day was very close to perfection.

The one easily forgiven flaw was a black girl seated by the net who'd set up a cluster of parasols to shield herself and her three-month old baby from the sun. O.K. for her and her baby, I suppose, but as for Marlene and I, and the several dozen people who sat near us, any close plays near the net were completely lost in the shade of her parasols.

Adding ants to the sand fleas, the black girl kept her back to the court most of the time. She had all the paraphernalia of the new mother, ointments and creams, bottles of formula that she kept mixing and exchanging, half a dozen baby outfits, diapers, baby powder, etc. Between changing her kid's clothing, feeding him, kissing him on the nose and cheeks, and tickling his tummy, I doubt whether she saw more than two or three minutes of each game.

"Isn't that little baby cute." Marlene says, and this just after the mother's activities had made us miss a close play at the net.

Two of the contestants, the muscular brunette and an equally broad-shouldered redhead on the opposite team, had fought for possession of the ball, fingertips grappling in mid-air. One had come down hard on the other's ankle, or so the other said, and the two were screaming at each other like ex-roommates.

The referee, a short, freckle-faced combination of Doris Day and Dennis the Menace, ended the impasse. Instead of intervening, she scooped the ball up from the sand and started volleying with someone in the crowd. The crowd roared. As for the brunette and the redhead, it's hard to stay angry when the crowd is laughing at you.

In the end, the screaming was unnecessary. The muscular brunette and her playmate partner won the semifinal handily, 15–6, 15–8. The low point was the frequent quarrels. The high point was when the two partners collided, sending Sara Newcombe, the playmate, sprawling deep in the sand.

How do you get sand out of your bathing suit with two hundred people looking on? Very carefully. Sara retrieved a large beach towel from her pile of belongings, carefully wrapped herself in the towel, loosened the sand-clogged folds of her suit and then carefully rotated back and forth while sand rained from under the towel ends. Gypsy Rose Lee couldn't have done it more discreetly and with greater effect on the male portion of the audience. But Marlene only said, "pigs," when I pointed out the obvious.

After the semifinal, the television camera crews moved in, roping off an area at each end for the cameras, setting up markers on the ground, and so forth. Most of the crowd, which had grown considerably since the early rounds of the tournament, used the opportunity to take a seventh-inning stretch. How much time could I spend stretching? With light checks and sound checks, the interval just stretched on and on.

"Want to take a walk along the beach?" I asked Marlene. A genteel snore was the only reply. Too much wine or maybe Marlene was just working on her tan.

I may have had a little too much wine myself. Picking my way through the crowd was like trying to walk across Pacific Coast Highway: beach blankets, Frisbee throwers, small children with sand pails, larger kids with ghetto blasters and boogie boards, paddle ball players—and those paddles are lethal. Just when I thought I'd found my way clear to the surf, I almost stepped into a line of kayaks drawn up at the water's edge.

The kayaks were part of the iron-man contest that Lackland Beer had running back-to-back with the volleyball tournament. If Lackland didn't get you watching the girls, they figured they would snag your attention with one of the long row of muscle-bound types that stood in a poised line waiting for the starter's gun.

I'm in pretty good shape myself—I'd once thought of competing as a bodybuilder—but these guys had to live for their bodies, judging by their bulging pects and the oil sheen on their backs and shoulders. Of course, it took more than muscle to win this iron-man contest. You had to be crazy, too. The race began with a 500-yard swim in rough surf—250 yards out and 250 yards back, followed by 750 yards paddling the kayaks through the same huge waves, and, finally, for those with time on their hands and a half hour or so to kill, a grueling 750 yards kneeling on surf boards, digging with both hands at the rough water.

Twenty yards from the start—a false start by the way—two of the contestants got wiped out by a wave, ate sand, and limped back into place. A second false start and a third of the muscular contestants was banished, shamefaced, never to return. That made three out of the contest and they hadn't even started! Given the size of the waves that day, they'd be lucky if anyone finished. Unfortunately, I never got to see the actual race, because a sustained cheer from behind me announced the volleyball finals were about to begin.

I ate a little sand myself getting back to my place at courtside. The crowds had gathered around the finals court like ants converging on a piece of fallen melon. I got nothing but hostile looks from the rows of bronzed surfers who stood in a wall outside the blankets. I tried to edge my way among them and was tripped a couple of times deliberately, once by a small girl. But make it back I did, only to be greeted with a chorus of "shhs" and "sit downs," before I could say a word.

The pair who'd won the last semifinal, Sara Newcombe and Erica Mueller—Sara the sexy blond, Erica the muscular brunette—were just starting to warm up. During the break, Sara had exchanged her gray bikini top for one of bright orange with the logo of her sponsor, Pacifica, a maker of suntan lotion, displayed in black across the front. The sponsor couldn't have picked a better location for the ad.

Erica had switched from a pale blue one-piece to one of a dazzling green. Perhaps the color matched her eyes. I wished she would smile more. More than ever, give or take a few pounds, Erica reminded me of the girl who had a locker next to mine in high school. She too could go from a smile to a frown in a fraction of a second. And I'd seen the effect the change had on anyone with the nerve to go up to her.

The black Madonna was still holding forth next to center court from beneath the shade of her parasols. The two remaining finalists and the referee were standing next to her, playing with the baby and taking generous swigs from their name-brand mineral water.

So this girl knew the players. Just who was she? I really resented her being there, holding down the very best spot at center court next to the net, taking up the players' time, and then not paying any attention to the game, herself.

"Just who is that black girl?"

Marlene looked at me as if I'd just stepped out of a space capsule. "That's Dee-Dee Williams," she said.

Dee-Dee Williams. And who in the hell is Dee-Dee Williams, I wondered, feeling just as ignorant as Marlene had hoped I would. Fortunately, the barrel-chested blond next to me whispered, "Just the number one female player in the entire world," to which a somewhat sunburned redhead sitting next to him added the single word, "Olympics."

Olympics. So the black girl was an Olympian, part of the team that had captured the silver medal for the U.S. I still thought she was rude.

The referee for the finals was the same freckled-faced kid whose relaxed friendly refereeing style we'd enjoyed so in the two previous matches. I noticed she used her hands a lot when she talked. And she seemed to bubble over with laughter. She laughed a lot during the games too, and joked with the players, trying to get them to forget what they were arguing about. Kind of the same approach a rodeo clown uses to distract a raging bull.

I wished her good luck with this approach in the tournament final. Beach volleyball players are supposed to call their own fouls, but, somehow, with money on the line, I didn't think she could rely much on tradition.

The two players the ref was joking with were an unlikely pair. One was tall—very tall, very elegant, and very blond, your All-American, California girl. Standing beside her, the referee resembled a whippet next to a greyhound. The tall blonde's partner, wearing an abbreviated bikini, was a dark-haired girl with dark-brown skin and a dazzling bright smile. She was shorter than the blonde's 6'2," but not short by any means, and was some kind of Central American—Cuban or Guatemalan.

"Who are they?" I asked.

"Just the tournament favorites," my friend said knowingly.

"That's Barbara Dahl and Chara deCastro." the barrel-chested surfer set me straight again. "Barb was on the '00 and '04 Olympic teams with Dee-Dee Williams. She's been beach women's champion now for three years in a row. Actually makes a living at it with all her endorsements. Probably the only female player that does. deCastro's new this year. She's a former member of the Cuban Olympic team. She'd be playing for them now except she pissed off some Commie bigwig."

"Doesn't speak English." someone else put in.

"Best players in the world." added a fourth person.

"The best two players in the world," whispered Marlene, "are Dee-Dee Williams, that black girl on the blanket next to us, and that tall handsome guy standing next to the T.V. commentator."

"He's . . ."

"He's Karch Kiraly. He's a hunk isn't he?"

"Seems kind of stringy to me."

"Mmph. Eat your melon."

Barbara Dahl didn't do as much for her swimsuit as Sara Newcombe did, but she had a certain class that made you think of Princess Di or Catherine DeNeueve. Her partner, deCastro, had no class at all. Her bikini even shocked me—

well almost. In action, deCastro reminded me of a stripper I'd seen once at an amateur night, running up and down the runway in high heels and a G-string, popping her gum and yelling, "whee!" Strictly off the wall.

deCastro's opening serve was strictly off the wall too, a high spinner that went thirty feet up into the air and came down kerplunk on her own side of the net.

"Best players in the world, uh," I said, as Erica and Sara took over.

The first three or four plays went the same way with deCastro and Dahl seemingly just warming up, while Erica and Sara made spectacular plays all over the court. Was an upset in the making?

Apparently, we weren't going to find out for a while. At a signal from a cameraman, the referee stopped play for a commercial break. Cries of outrage came from all around the court. Was beach volleyball to be yet another captive of the tube? Of course it was, but this didn't make the crowd any happier.

The players seemed to take the pause in stride, either swigging mineral water in the shade of Dee-Dee William's umbrellas, or standing in the bright sun joking with the referee.

When play resumed, it followed more or less the same pattern: deCastro and Dahl relaxed and easy, Erica and Sara hustling for every ball. Surprisingly, given the unmatched nature of the action, the score was tied 8–8 and remained tied after half a dozen side outs.

"What's going on?" I asked Marlene.

"Barb and Chara make the points when they need them."

My turn to say, "Hmphf."

By the time the cameraman signaled for a second commercial, brunette and friend looked somewhat the worse for wear. As Marlene had observed so acutely, Dahl and deCastro were making the points when they needed them. Erica and Sara were not scoring when they had the serve, or, if they did score, it was only after a long, drawn out rally in which one or the other had made a spectacular but exhausting play.

Professional volleyball is not exactly the game you play at the church picnic. All sorts of rules cover the handling of the ball. The players are supposed to call their own fouls, but there's always room for argument. Was it a clean pass or wasn't it? Did the player touch the net or didn't she? Apparently, Erica Mueller didn't think the other team was calling their own fouls. And she knew the ref wasn't. The more points Erica and her partner lost, the more she screamed at her opponents. Once I thought she was going to physically attack Barbara Dahl for whom she seemed to have a special hatred.

Of course, this didn't set well with the crowd at all. Princess Di cheat? No way. The referee must have thought so too, for she just kept smiling in the face of Erica's insults while Dahl and deCastro piled up the score.

Another commercial break. Barbara Dahl tossed back half a flask of imported bottled water, the product of one of her many sponsors, while Erica strode up and down her end of the court like some avenging fury.

It was still a close game, 17–15, when the difference between champion quality and spectacular effort was made plain. deCastro delivered another of her crazy up-in-the air serves and Erica missed it completely. She started to argue, but this time even her partner told her to shut up. With Sara and Erica quarreling, the score quickly went from 27–25 to 29–25 in Dahl and deCastro's favor. One more point and the match would be over.

As the scorer flipped the card with the 29 on its front, Erica had sense enough to take another little stroll around her backcourt. Long enough to regain some of her class, but not enough to get her second wind, alas. The last point, a long, long rally ended with Erica face down in the sand pounding her fists like a child, while the crowd swooped down to congratulate her grinning opponents.

From where I sat, you could see deCastro was beaming from ear to ear. Barbara kept leaping into the air as if replaying her last wonderful game-winning spike over and over. The camera crew got through to them finally—the crowd just wouldn't give way—and Barbara took a final sip from the bottled water before turning to the interviewer. Then in full sight of the crowd, the hundreds on the beach, and the tens of thousands who would be watching when the action was replayed on T.V., Barbara clutched at her stomach, doubled over, and collapsed dead on the sand.

Chapter 2

The people around us started to get up and rush forward, thought better of it, and then sat back down again. The ones standing in the back oscillated to and fro, some talking, some, the talkative ones, more silent than they ever had been. Only a few hardy souls gathered up their blankets and their parasols and started the slow trudge toward the parking lot.

Marlene, that very special person of mine sat very still, holding my hand and, I think, crying while we waited for someone in authority to tell us that what had happened had not happened after all. "She's dead," Marlene said, wanting me to tell her, that no, Barbara was not dead. But I was sure she was.

I'd been sure she was dead when I saw the way she crumpled to the ground, like a gracious dying bird, its wing feathers heavy with oil. And what convinced me that Barbara was dead was that no one, absolutely no one, had rushed forward and tried to comfort her since the initial scramble. No one was sitting next to Barbara talking quietly to her the way you would with someone who had just fainted or was injured and waiting for the ambulance. Instead, the other players kept their distance, standing in little clusters whispering. One or two of the players hugged each other, but no one spoke.

I think the freckle-faced referee may have gone up once and touched Barbara's prone figure; I'd seen her down on one knee beside Chris Marlowe, the announcer, holding Barbara's wrist and counting. Chris had come over because he'd been doing the play-by-play of the game for ESPN and had been going to do the interview with Barbara afterward. But mostly the media people and the tournament officials waited off by the sidelines as we did for someone in authority to tell us what to do.

I wished that someone would go over and cover her body with a towel. It wasn't just that Barbara had been a symbol of all that was good about the game, it was that a few moments before she had been as warm, as vibrant, as healthy as any one of us. I was having too many unhappy thoughts about my own mortality. I think all of us were.

The police were a long time in coming. Just before they arrived, one of the iron-man contestants, still dripping from the surf, broke through the waiting crowd. He was a big man, with the well-developed muscles of a weight lifter. With a sound somewhere between a cry and a bellow, he threw himself on Barbara's crumpled form.

She looked so tiny in his arms. Barbara Dahl had been six feet one, six feet two in life. Now she lay limp and small as if she were some kind of a rag doll.

He was crying. He kept trying to give Barbara artificial respiration as if somehow he thought she had drowned, but his crying prevented him. Then two of the women, Erica Mueller and someone else from the group of players, led him away. He was still standing off to the side sobbing questions, "My God, what happened? Can't somebody tell me what happened?" when the police finally came.

If you thought that because I'm a private detective I spent any particular amount of time the next day speculating about Barbara Dahl's murder, then you're wrong. The police are paid to solve crimes. They have the manpower to interview the 400 odd spectators, passersby, Frisbee throwers, etc. present at the scene, any one of whom might have had the motive and the opportunity. Even then the police might not have the answers for several days or ever depending on how the clever the killer had been.

Like everyone else, I'd seen Barbara taking that last drink and falling over and over again on the TV news, but I still had no idea what had really happened. "It was poison wasn't it?" I asked Marvin the Account Rep, when he showed up at my office unexpectedly the next day.

Marvin had all the answers. "Yeah. It was poison all right. They found strychnine in the water bottle. Gezmuller water for your health. Can you imagine? Gezmuller is one of our biggest sponsors.

They'll be ruined. Volleyball will be ruined. Now you know why I'm here."

"I'm not exactly sure why you're here," I told Marvin pointedly, "I'm a private investigator but the police..."

But Marvin (I never did learn his last name and maybe I didn't care) was already plunging ahead without me. Marvin didn't take no for an answer. Marvin couldn't hear the "no" as Marvin didn't listen.

To be frank, Marvin the Account Rep kind of made a bad first, second, and third impression on me. It was a question of style. Marvin's style was modeled on some ancient Greek despot patronizing a distant relative. His cocky walk—he was a short little guy—his puffed up chest, and an irritating habit of beating at his thigh with a gold pen as if the pen were a riding crop, suggested that his own personal role model was General George Patton.

Marvin (Marv?) lived in a world of first names—Morgan, and Larry, and Dee-Dee, and Bill. Some were in show business, some venture capital, some played volleyball. If Marvin were to be believed, all had in common that they did not eat, sleep, invest, marry, or purchase the morning paper without first consulting or confiding in Marvin.

Had Marvin the affability of a salesperson, I'd have found him marginally tolerable. But he didn't. Put him down as kind of a pompous combination of Laura (Dr.), Russ (Limbaugh) and Howard (Cosell). (See, I can drop names, too.)

Marvin was definitely not a beach type, with his salon blow-dried hair, horn rim glasses and three-piece suit—vest matching. (At least he didn't wear gold chains). But he was directly responsible for the Professional Volleyball Association and its current, record high six million dollar account.

"Six million dollars?" I gasped.

"Six million dollars."

There was a pause as both of us began to wonder why a guy with a six million a year account would be interested in a bottom-of-the-line P.I. like me.

I don't work out of a high rent neighborhood. I'm near the docks, in fact, so I can dash down and do a little fishing. I don't have a display ad in the yellow pages. When a corporate exec wants discreet inquires, he doesn't punch me up with his computerized dialer. I get delivered along with your canteen supplies and plastic forks. Three hundred dollars a day and I'll settle for two fifty, if you guarantee me a week's work.

I knew Marvin's firm had an investigator on retainer, in fact they had an entire agency, one of the biggest agencies in town. It was one of these agents, a guy I'd flunked out of the police academy with years before, who'd spotted me on the films they had borrowed from the local T.V. station.

As Marvin put it, less than tactfully, "We're hiring you because one of my guys spotted you in the crowd. You were the only P.I. in the book who was sitting on the beach yesterday not four feet from where the murder was committed."

You can't often count on that degree of specialization in my business. Then again, if the entire murder was on film, suspects included, that was all the more reason the police could handle it, and I told Marvin so. "Wrong again," Marvin told me, "The films merely cut down the number of suspects to 50 instead of 450 people.

"And the worst part is that they're all connected in some way with professional volleyball.

"Do you know how much suspicion that generates? I don't mean with the public, all the press about the murder has been real good for us, I mean the players are all upset and suspicious. The players are suspicious of one another, they're suspicious of the managers, they're suspicious of the promoters.

"Do you how many calls I got last night *after* I went to bed?" And here Marvin was off again on another orgy of names that I didn't recognize but that avid readers of Sports Illustrated, People, and the National Enquirer would probably have got right off the bat.

The bottom line, as Marvin explained it to me, and Marvin, I knew by then, dealt only in bottom lines, was that while professional volleyball looked to be very, very big long term, right now it was on a shoestring budget. "$2600 first prize," Marvin said. "That's what Barb and Chara got to split for winning the tournament. Can you believe it? Would you play golf for $2600?"

I would, but I got the point. It was hope for the future and sheer love of the game that kept the professionals going. And trust, Marvin said.

"We're a family, O.K. A family is built on trust. Take that trust away, make the players suspicious of one another, and it all goes down the tubes.

"You keep talking about the police. But there's one and only one reason I'm here in your office that, by the way, needs an interior decorator. We want someone to check into this situation quickly, quietly, and discreetly. Just like it says on your business cards. Someone who knows something about volleyball. Someone who can do a job ."

"But the police . . ." I tried interrupting him once more.

"What we don't need are the police, stepping on everybody's toes, raking up old animosities. Of course, the police are going to investigate. We can't do much about that. What we can do is have you cover the same ground, but quickly and quietly. You solve the murder, the police make the bust, no more suspicion."

"We all live happily ever after?"

"And I get my ten percent." He wasn't joking.

I must have been eating stupid pills not to have taken his money then and there, but still all I could see were the objections. "Suppose I need backup. The police have already assigned three or four detectives to the case."

"Be real. The police have only assigned one guy, a detective named Carpenter. He's new and he's already got a heavy caseload. You need backup? I'm your backup. You get a hot lead? You call me."

Marvin stepped back and took a long hard look at me as if seeing me for the first time.

"Money. It's money isn't it? You're worried about money."

"No. No, I'm . . . ."

"I'm going to write you a big check. Now. I'm going to write you a second big check later. Soon as you solve the murder."

"But. . ."

"You find the murderer you come to me."

"But we're going to have to tell the police sooner or later."

Marvin gave me the look old time Greek tyrants reserved for imbecile relatives. He wrote the check. He handed it to me.

I glanced at the check. About two thousand dollars more than I'd expected and almost as much as I'd taken in during the past two months.

"Naturally," Marvin said, "there will be a second check just like this one once you identify the murderer."

My mouth opened. Words came out. "But if we know who did it, we've got to tell the police." Who said that? Did I say that? I needed the money. I couldn't afford not to do what Marvin said. Fortunately, though Marvin had listened, he still hadn't heard me.

"And if you're wrong?" he said. "I'm paying for quickly, quietly, and discreetly like it says on your business cards. Have we got a deal?"

And that's how Faust sold his soul to the devil. Me too.

Chapter 3

The long-distance monologue that followed Marvin's presentation of the check was every bit as boring as the long-distance monologue he'd delivered earlier and it covered much the same ground—Marvin's accomplishments as testified to by Jane, Clint, and Karch Kiraly, Marvin's early career, Marvin's prospects, even Marvin's likely choice of a date for the evening. Little about Barbara and the possible suspects in her murder. Nothing I could use in the investigation. In fact, it was only as an afterthought that Marvin handed me the list.

"I've left you the names of the five prime suspects," he said. "I'm sure you'll find that one of them is the killer." With that Marvin left finally, leaving only the reek of his cologne in my office.

I unfolded the piece of paper I'd been handed. Five names were neatly typed on a sheet of Marvin's embossed letterhead, the results, I suppose of a morning's brainstorming session at his agency: Erica Mueller, Diane Purdy, Sara Newcombe, JoAnne Greene and Derek Chzynski. Choose one as a murderess or murderer of beach volleyball's leading woman player.

Three of the names on the list I recognized: Erica Mueller, Sara Newcombe, and JoAnne Greene. Erica Mueller, she of the bright green bathing suit and the bad manners, had been Barbara's opponent in the finals. She had spent most of the game threatening her opponents and the referee. I could see why she was a suspect and marked her down for an early interview.

Sara Newcombe was the blond with the playmate figure. She'd been Erica's partner in the tournament and had done her best to keep Erica from losing her temper. Definitely not my notion of a murderer, but with her figure, she too was a must for an interview. Maybe later.

JoAnne Greene was a well-known media personality—at least to volleyball fans. Brought in the previous year to substitute for one of the regular ESPN commentators, she'd gone on to be the permanent replacement. She'd played and coached in college. She'd even played beach volleyball at one time, although those days were long past.

JoAnne wasn't an Angela Joli for looks, but she was a Mary Tyler-Moore for personality. Pleasant and extremely knowledgeable. As with Harry Cary the late baseball announcer, listening to JoAnne was almost as much fun as watching the game itself. She always had something to contribute. A murder suspect? No way. But she knew as much about pro volleyball and the players as anyone did and, because I'd always wanted to meet JoAnne, I decided to start with her.

The drive through the nearby college town where JoAnne lived was the usual stop and go with students crossing the street at random with little regard to the signal instructions. Spree bikes with skimpily dressed riders predominated and in my ancient Plymouth coupe I was an evident intruder.

A positive note was a new Top Dog franchise that featured five different types of hot dogs, from Native Americans—your Chicago dog and Louisiana red hot, to exotic European breeds like bratwurst and knaacksad. I marked the stand down for a possible later visit. I'm not a taste-a-vin gourmet, but I do like my food.

I was eager to meet JoAnne. On the tube, she came across as a relaxed easygoing individual whom you would like the instant you met. Over the telephone and later on our first contact in the living room of her town house, she came across the same way. If she wasn't Mary Tyler Moore, she was Mary's mother, and I could tell at a glance where Mary got her personality.

JoAnne's house was located in a quiet area near the University, though a small spot of domestic violence marked my arrival. Through my window I could see him, yelling back into the open doorway before he stomped off furiously to his car. She followed a scant instant later, slamming the door behind her, and yelling something equally inaudible in reply. He backed furiously out of his driveway at three times the speed approved by the local vehicle code, narrowly missing my front fender. An instant later, she got in her car and did the same thing. I parked. Life in suburbia was too rough for me.

The interview didn't go the way I expected. It wasn't JoAnne's fault. It was the fault of the seven angry women I found seated on the couch in her living room. All somewhere in their early or late twenties, all dressed like JoAnne in collegiate casual, sweat shirts and baggy pants, with a glint of gold chains underneath. Her students and ex-students I imagined, though nobody actually introduced us.

I'd sort of slipped in JoAnne's front door when no one answered my knock. Her house was located midway along the row of identical town houses, and I'd almost walked by it. Even then I wasn't sure I had the right address. It was that kind of neighborhood. Some kind of party going on inside—lots of talk and laughter. But the noise came to an abrupt halt as soon as I put my head in the door. Seven faces gave me swift looks of disapproval. Seven pairs of steely eyes followed my walk from the front door to the living room. And of course, all this time I'm thinking, could I be in the wrong house?

JoAnne was the one familiar landmark, and I greeted her with relief. JoAnne is not the sort of person you can overlook even if you have never seen her on the tube. She's stocky to begin with, and her laughter makes her seem larger than she really is. Once we'd established I was not a prowler, she gave me a big hello and even a half hug just the way I'd imagined she would. "Hey guys, this is someone, what's your name again?"

"Phyllis Ludwigsohn."

"Ok, Phyll, who needs to talk to me about Barbara."

We began talking away a mile a minute just as if we were old friends instead of two people who'd met on the phone only a half hour or so earlier. We talked about her appearances on T.V. and games we'd both seen and which teams looked good this year. She knew the people we talked about; I knew about them. The interview should have been both the beginning and the end of my investigation. But what's wrong with the picture is the seven pairs of silent staring eyes and the general air of hostility like the Charles Manson family at bay. I guess Jesse Jackson felt the same way the first time he was introduced to George Bush.

I had lots I wanted to say, but I soon ran out of words. It's hard to talk with someone face to face when every nerve in your body is telling you to look back over your shoulder. And the silence only made things worse.

This goony looking star child on the couch, all mascara and eye shadow, nineteen or twenty and probably the youngest one in the room, is the first to speak up. She turns to me and asks, "How do you know JoAnne?"

"Everyone knows JoAnne," I reply, "She's a media personality."

Then the chick turns to JoAnne and asks her, "Why is he talking to you?"

"He's a friend of Marvin."

After which the chick settles back to giving me the hate stare along with her six friends.

"JoAnne," I ask, "can we go somewhere so we can talk alone?"

"Will it take long?" JoAnne beams. I know she's on my side, but. . .

"Just a few questions. I need to go over the list of suspects with you."

"No problem, come on in the kitchen."

JoAnne leads me through the newly painted swinging door into a white-walled kitchen, immaculate, yet lived in like the rest of her house. I'm glad to get away from the hate squad, but the weird looking girl is only a step or two behind us.

JoAnne gestures toward the table, a breakfast nook separated by a counter from the main part of the kitchen, but it's the girl who takes a seat. I stand awkwardly while JoAnne gets two bottles of mineral water from the refrigerator and puts them onto the table. "Open these will you," she says to the girl.

We both stand waiting while the girl fetches two glasses, fills one with mineral water and hands it JoAnne, then fills the second glass and sits down to drink it herself.

"So how can I help you?" JoAnne asks.

There is a pause while I clear my throat thirstily, then I begin. "Marvin gave me the name of five, uh four people, he thought might be suspects in the case. I was sorta of hoping you could give me a little background on each one. In private?

She doesn't move. I continue. "Like I said, I've watched you on television, and you really come across like someone who knows the game and the players. It would be really good for volleyball if we could close this case in a hurry. I'm hoping you can help me get a handle on the suspects' personalities, their likes and dislikes."

"Well thank you, I'll see what I can do," JoAnne says. The weird chick merely gives me a hard stare.

"Uh, the first one is Erica Mueller."

"Erica Mueller? Hard worker, lots of energy. She was one of the founders of the Women's Association. Really put her heart into it. A little hard to get along with sometimes, which is maybe why she's no longer one of the officers. And, oh yes, a great competitor."

"Do you know of any reason why she would want Barbara dead?

"No."

"Do you think she killed Barbara?"

"Probably not."

"Sara Newcombe."

"Hah." This from the weird chick who has been making a steady stream of faces throughout the conversation.

"One of the best young players in the country. Strong competitor. Good figure also which really turns on some of the guys."

The weird chick makes another noise in her throat and JoAnne finally turns to her, "Look Deb, why don't you beat it. Go review the new rotation so we can work on it later this afternoon." She smiled indulgently as she said to me, "Typical California airhead. Sara beat her out for a slot on my team five years ago and she's still mad."

"Your team?" I hadn't thought of JoAnne as a coach, though I suppose it was obvious.

"My team. I coach too you know. College and club both. Sara was one of my best players at one time." (And to the girl again.) "And you're one of my best players now, Deborah. O.K. Now run along."

Deborah doesn't move. The whole situation reminds me of a divorced mother I knew with three impossible children all of whom she loved a lot more than any guy or girl. The mom still doesn't have a partner as far as I know.

"What was Sara's connection with Barbara?" I ask.

"You know, for awhile I thought they were going to pair up this year on the beach volleyball circuit. But then Chara deCastro came along."

"de Castro? She the dark-skinned girl who was Barbara's partner in the tournament?"

"Yea. She used to play on the Cuban Olympic team, until she defected to this country. I suppose she's on your suspect list, too."

I shook my head.

"Well she should be. They say Barbara was robbing her blind."

"Can't even speak English." This from the girl.

"Neither can you dear. Sometimes I wonder how you ever made it through college."

"Athletic scholarship."

"Yes dear, I know." JoAnne gave me another of those what can you do about it looks. I thought, maybe chase the kid away so we can get some work done, but I didn't say what I was thinking. JoAnne clearly wasn't going to make a move in that direction.

"Who else is on your list?" she asks.

"Diane Purdy. I'm not even sure who she is."

"She thinks she's Doris Day." This time the voice came from behind me. A tall blond girl dressed in baggy blue sweats had popped her head into the doorway about a head and a half above where you normally would expect a woman's head to be. So now there were two of the Manson family listening in. I wondered how long it would take before the entire group put in an appearance.

“Diane is another great competitor,” JoAnne began. “She’s kind of short for the pro circuit, but she really makes it up for it in hustle.”

“No, no,” I interrupted, “I mean who is she? How does she fit into the picture? Was she Barbara’s trainer or what?”

“Diane refereed the finals.”

Now it came to me. The sassy girl with the freckles who’d laughed everybody through the tense moments. Doris Day. Yeah, that description really fit. Diane (and Doris) were proof Hugh Heffner is right, it’s the ones that look like the girl next door who are the sexiest.

“Why would she want to kill Barbara?” I asked.

“Why would anyone want to kill Barbie?” mimicked two voices behind me in the doorway. “She was a slut.”

Realizing I was hearing something that might be important, I asked to no one in particular, “Was she sleeping around?”

“Yea,” came a choir of voices.

JoAnne laughed, “Will you be quiet. This man will get a terrible impression of us. No, to be frank, I don’t think Diane killed Barbara.”

“So far you don’t think anyone killed Barbara.”

“Except maybe deCastro.”

Who is not on my list, I thought. “Last chance, Derek Chzynski.”

“Hah.” This time the laughter was general. “Not a chance, Barbara led him around by the muscles.”

“Sides, his momma wouldn’t let him play with weapons.” This from the blond in the doorway.

“Sides, he didn’t have a weapon,” this from two more voices behind the blond.

“O.K., guys,” JoAnne interjects, “Let me answer the questions. All right?”

"Thanks." I say and I mean it. "Maybe you could give me a little background on Barbara herself."

"Not much I can add to what Marvin already told you or what I said on T.V.She was a great competitor and a natural leader. She's always been the sort of person younger players would look up to, the sort of person a coach would want on her team."

"That's more or less what you said on T.V."

"Yes."

"Is there anything else?"

"There's Barbara's Kids of course."

A chorus of snorts came from the door behind me.

"Barbara really tried to do good in her way."

"But your girls seem to feel, they suggested . . ."

"Oh, pooh. They're jealous. I think we all were jealous of Barbara's success. It's hard not to when you consider she was a relative newcomer."

"She'd been playing beach ball for nearly five years!" I had to ask myself why I was so hotheaded, why I was defending a woman I'd never met.

"Oh you know what I mean," Joanne said, and she crossed her arms for the first time in our conversation.

"O.K.," I said recovering. I did not want to offend her; she was still my best source of inside information. "Derek Chzynski didn't kill Barbara, nor did Erica Mueller, Sara, or Diane. Any other suggestions?"

JoAnne shrugged. "Nope. I don't think so." Her arms were still crossed. Clearly, she thought the interview was over.

Then that really leaves only you, I thought, or deCastro.

"Did you do it?" I asked. JoAnne laughed. The laugh should have been and was intended to be infectious, but I persisted, "Did you kill Barbara Dahl? Where were you during the final matches?"

"She was with me," a half dozen voices answered. By this time, the entire Manson family had piled into the kitchen. The vibes were as hostile as they'd been when I first arrived.

"I was sitting with my friends," JoAnne said, "Marlowe was handling the telecast."

"Marlowe?"

"Chris Marlowe, the guy I usually do the games with, used to be captain of the men's Olympic team."

The announcer. I knew who he was. Marcelled hairdo. Profile for the camera. He'd been the first to reach Barbara after she fell. But that was after she fell. I had a sudden inspiration. "What about the black chick that was watching the game from center court with her little boy."

"The black what," a half dozen voices wanted to know. The vibe in the kitchen got still more hostile, if that were possible.

"The black girl," I stammered, "I mean the black woman. The one on the blanket."

"Thank you," JoAnne said, "that was Dee-Dee Williams."

I knew that. What I wanted to know was how Dee-Dee and Barbara had gotten along. What I wanted was to talk to JoAnne alone, for half an hour, like I'd imagined I would when I first called her up.

The weird chick was holding open the back door so I could leave. The rest of the Manson family pressed close behind me. So I left. Quickly. I had ran afoul of a group of girls in the third grade once; something to do with my talking out of turn and the teacher punishing the entire class by canceling our painting period; those girls beat the hell out of me.

Ten minutes later, I emerged from the alleyway behind the row of townhouses where Erica's players had let me out. They might have noticed I couldn't get directly back to the street that way. It took a block and a half of back-alley walking before I could retrieve my car. No trouble; I stay in shape.

Only the Capezios I'd put on specially for JoAnne had problems.

So now I know that Erica Mueller is a great competitor, so is Sara Newcombe, and so is Doris Day, that is, Diane Purdy, volleyball player and volleyball referee. As for Derek Chzynski, Barbara's fiancée, a natural strongman who could probably have ripped a telephone book apart with his hands, he was just a little boy whom Barbara had led around by the muscles. That left nobody as a real murder suspect, unless you counted the Cuban defector Chara deCastro. And one more person.

I'd lied to JoAnne. There hadn't been four names on Marvin's list; there'd been five. And the fifth was my new number one suspect, JoAnne Greene.

Chapter 4

It took a ham sandwich—Virginia country with plenty of hot mustard, and a beer from the Trader's—Groetz Pilsner from Czechoslovakia, very tasty and as the Trader says a lot less than you'd pay at the supermarket—before I even began to feel whole again. I'd have liked a turkey sandwich, too, but there were about three months to go before leftover season.

The interview with JoAnne had taken a lot out of me and my clothes, both. The Capezios I'd worn to the meeting—I normally favor a pair of Nikes—were scuffed beyond repair. My dressy slacks I tossed into a heap by the front door for the cleaners. Too much back alley work.

And yet what had I learned? Nothing concrete, just something bad about almost everyone connected with the case. Despite JoAnne's seeming endless good cheer, there'd been an edge to each of her compliments. Erica Mueller, a wonderful person, was hard to get along with. Diane Purdy, the great competitor, was too short for the pro circuit. And so on and so on. My brother's ex-wife had been much the same way, all sunbeams on the outside, all knife work if you got in too close.

I hoped Erica Mueller, the next one on my list, was a straight shooter. It was time I had some hard answers to my questions.

Erica Mueller was one of those women who look better with her clothes on. A lot better. Excess flesh gets tucked away beneath the folds. Out come the nail polish, the lipstick, and the accessories. The eye and the nose of the beholder are bewitched and distracted. I liked what I saw.

Erica was in her mid to late thirties. Because of that, the other players called her Grandma. Well, Grandma had very shapely legs and calves encased in carefully tailored Liz Claiborne slacks. Grandma's bosom amply filled her matching Liz Claiborne blouse and strained against the buttons. Grandma had frosted fingernails of light coral and deeper coral lips. Even Grandma's feet looked sexy in open-toed sandals. It wasn't quite the way I remembered her looking on the beach, but they touch up playmates of the month with an airbrush don't they?

The only distraction was a dog or a cat that was prowling at the rear of Erica's small apartment which like Erica, herself, (grandma, if you prefer), showed a lot of class. Within the limits of a J.C. Penny budget, Santa Fe colors of peach, gray and tan accented the room. The big throw pillows on her couch—they looked hand-woven, they felt like cotton—were beginning to feel very comfortable. Definitely a comfortable room decorated by a caring woman.

I listened again. Yes, someone or something was moving about in the adjoining room. I just hoped it wasn't a male companion. Erica and I were beginning to feel very comfortable as a twosome. What I hoped must have shown in my face—I never could play poker—and Erica was on her feet in an instant.

"It's time to wrap up this interview, Ms. Ludwigson. I didn't invite you in to devour me with your eyes. If you have questions to ask me. Ask them now."

Wow! Not what I intended. Things couldn't have gone wronger. Erica stood up from the couch, her bosom a ship's prow, and in less time than it had taken me to walk from the front door to her couch I was back at the front door again.

"Now wait a minute," I stammered, "I still have questions."

“Ask them. You have two minutes.” And, so help me, she took off her wristwatch and held it up pointedly in front of my face.

The interview had started out on a relatively friendly basis despite the frosty reception she’d given my original telephone call. Apparently, between the time I telephoned and the time I arrived at her apartment, Erica had called Marvin or Marvin had called Erica. I’d gotten a warm smile from her at the door, a comfortable seat on her couch, and a hot cup of coffee, fresh, not instant.

In fact, we were side by side on the overstuffed couch, two woman wondering if the attraction were mutual, when I let my extended adolescence betray me. Now I was face to face in a narrow hallway with 150 pounds of angry female. And so help me, I loved every minute of it.

Besides her perfume was sexy as hell.

“You, Ms. Ludwigsohn are a pig.”

“And you, Ms. Mueller, are a murder suspect. You threatened Barbara Dahl’s life on the court yesterday. I heard you; I was only three or four feet away. You called her a bitch.”

“Under my breath.”

“I can lip-read, Ms Mueller. We all can lip-read.”

Whatever sympathy the crowd may have had that sunny Sunday afternoon for Erica Mueller and her partner as underdogs, that sympathy soon vanished in the face of Erica’s foul mouth and bad temper. True, one or two close calls could have been argued either way. but as the score began to pile up against her, Erica had launched an endless barrage of abuse that first amused and then annoyed the crowd. There’d even been one entire time out, off camera during a commercial break, in which Erica had walked about the court kicking at the sand, yelling to the world, “that bitch.”

As I reviewed her behavior on the court, Erica had the grace to look embarrassed... momentarily, of course. "I'm very competitive," she said.

"People have told me that. But I think you went beyond the bounds of competition last Sunday."

Again, she gave me that apologetic little girl look that I think is done best by tall full-figured women like Erica. Can you imagine 150 pounds of woman melting in your arms? I can. Maybe I was getting somewhere, after all. I heard a noise, noises from the back of her apartment in the direction of her bedroom. Someone was taking a shower and it definitely wasn't a cat. Who else lived here? Husband? Live-in boyfriend?

Erica kept talking. Was she trying to cover up the sounds? "Look, I'm an intense player. Besides, I really don't give a damn what you think, Ms. Ludwigsohn. I might have kicked that bitch's ankle one or two times under the net if I thought I could get away with it, but I wasn't going to poison her. Sara and I were going to have too much fun beating them in the next tournament."

I doubt that, I though privately. Following Erica's last temper tantrum, Barbara's partner had served three straight aces into their court. One, two, three the game was over. The general impression was that Barbara and Chara had been toying with Erica and her partner the entire time. From the expression of rage on Erica's face, I could see she was thinking the same thing.

I took a shot in the dark. "This isn't the first time you've threatened Barbara's life, is it?"

Erica's face turned almost purple with rage, but she held her temper and her tongue. Talk, I prayed to whatever saint watches over private detectives. Lose your temper Erica and talk.

We stood toe to toe, her slate green eyes only inches from my battered brown ones, her coarse features marked indelibly on my mind. I tired to look everywhere but straight ahead, but those eyes wouldn't let me. There was a hint of two taloned fists just waiting to work me over. God, she was attractive.

More noises came from the back of the apartment. The shower had stopped now and someone was making himself or herself at home in the bedroom, opening and shutting closets and slamming bureau drawers.

"I still need to ask you a few more questions," I stammered, trying to think of the questions I needed to ask. I've never been good at thinking on my feet and this close to Erica I found it hard to think at all.

"Make it quick." Her breath was like peaches. Why was I always attracted to the bossy type?

"Tell me about beach volleyball?"

"A very popular summertime sport demanding great agility, power, and split-second timing. Enjoyed by millions but mainly played by the same people who played volleyball in college and who now are hopefuls in the pro circuit."

"How did you first get interested?" (What was I, a junior high school reporter? At least my questions were keeping the conversation going.)

"I played Division I volleyball at UCLA, majored in phys ed and coached both women and men's volleyball at Orange Coast College. I've coached there for nine years and have won three local championships and one national. Is that all?"

"Almost all. Almost all. I've got a few people I want to ask you about." Her green eyes still locked me in place. Her lips were only a few inches away, her breath still smelling of peaches. God, she was a gorgeous woman.

The list of suspects. Where had I put the list? "Diane Purdy?" I asked.

"A suburban housefrau."

"Derek Chzynski?"

"An ape man."

"JoAnne Greene?"

"A hypocrite."

At least, we agreed on something. "Sara Newcombe?"

"Sara is a friend as well as a partner."

"A friend who used to play for your college club?"

"I never select my friends from my players unlike certain other people."

"Like JoAnne Greene?"

"If you say so."

"Who killed Barbara Dahl?"

"Nobody."

"Nobody?"

"She wasn't worth it."

"Nobody put the poison in the bottle?"

"Somebody put the poison in the bottle. But it just wasn't one of us. It wasn't me. It wasn't Sara. It probably wasn't anyone connected with beach volleyball. It could have been any of a hundred other people whom Barbara fucked over with her mean manipulative ways. Time's up, Ms. Ludwigsohn. Are you quite through asking questions?"

The dismissal was tossed in so abruptly I was caught off guard once again. Which of us was supposed to be putting the other on the spot? I had to stall for time. There were too many questions I needed to ask her, now. Who were these other people who had wanted Barbara dead? And why? Had any of them had the opportunity to put poison in the water bottle?

"Then, goodbye." Erica said.

Wait! Give me a chance, I thought frantically. "Ah, I may have to see you again."

"Goodbye."

The door to the bedroom opened revealing the source of the noises. It was Sara Newcombe, all five feet, eleven inches of her partially wrapped in two bath towels, one around her hair, the other held by one arm around her middle covering roughly the area from her nipples to her mid thigh.

Sara saw me gaping and smiled. Erica reacted by slamming the front door against the wall, bashing my knee as I scrambled to get out of the way. “Get out,” she screamed.

I got out. The apartment door slammed shut behind me leaving me in a maze of virtually identical doorways. I went left. More corridors and more doorways. I went right. The same.

I’d found Erica’s apartment the first time only because Erica was holding the door open for me. Now, I was lost. I may have passed Erica and Sara’s door a half dozen times in the next ten minutes or I may have been off in a completely different corner of the building. Who knew? Finally, I made it down the stairs and out the front door. Fortunately, nobody saw me leave. For the second time that day, I was out on the street with a bruised ego and a whole new series of unanswered questions.

Erica and Sara?

Chapter 5

Did you ever have the feeling that someone was following you? Just because I'm paranoid doesn't mean they're not out to get me.

I had a strong feeling someone was behind me, and that they'd been behind me, just out of my line of sight all day. And that's not the way it's supposed to be. Normally, I follow people, a two-timing husband, or an errant employee on her way to fence the materials she's stolen from her boss' warehouse. I'm very good at following. Usually, the person I'm tailing never even looks up. But ever since I'd left Erica's apartment, I'd been looking up, around, and all about me. I hadn't seen anybody, but I was 100% sure there was someone out there tailing me, first on foot, and then in a car. And I kept reminding myself this was a murder investigation.

He (or she) had picked me up shortly after I left Erica's apartment building. They were waiting on the opposite side of the street, following and not following me until I got to my car. When I looked in the rearview mirror, they were gone. Crazy, right? But someone had been there and I knew that same someone was still following me after I cut back into traffic, even though I couldn't have told you which car they were in.

One of the reasons I'm so good as a tail is because of something I learned while in the service. Right there in the infantryman's manual it says, "If hiding in ambush, never look directly at the enemy. He will soon become conscious of your presence." So I never do. On maneuvers, I'd look at the trees. Now, I look into store windows or at street signs. But the person behind me hadn't read the manual. They were looking at me and their eyes continued to bore into my back all the way from Erica's apartment until I got back to my office.

Only in the hall of my office building did I feel free of the unseen figure's presence, though I was willing to bet that somewhere outside, parked in traffic, he or she was still waiting and watching. But who? And why?

That someone had been in my office! I knew it the instant I stepped inside the door. And no, it wasn't easy to be sure of this either.

There isn't very much in my office, but what little there is is not very tidy if you know what I mean.

I've a chair, a desk, and a gooseneck desk lamp. There's a pile of clothes next to the hat rack and a surfboard in the far corner. Some days, I'll come in wearing jeans and switch to shorts if it gets hotter; some days when the fog rolls in around four p.m., it's the other way around. There's no plan to it.

Half a dozen empty hangers cling to an otherwise empty hat rack. That's because I'll pick up my stuff at the cleaners before a meeting and come back here to change. The old clothes go on the floor. With luck, I'll remember to take them back to the house before I do the laundry.

But whoever had been searching my office, hadn't been going through my old clothes. They hadn't been going through the papers on my desk either. For once, my desktop was clean. Sort of. There were a few doodles I'd put together while listening to Marvin: A guy's big nose protruding through a knot hole in a fence, a stick-figure woman slapping a stick-figure man's face. I think the notepad had been moved; it just wasn't dusty enough.

The list of names Marvin had given me was still in my pocket, assuming it was the list they were after.

I checked the desk drawers. Sweat socks, spare trunks, old keys, shoehorn, parking stubs. Blank, very elegant stationery in another drawer. The stationery has a pen drawing of a huge vigilant eye in one corner. Get it? I don't think it was a very good idea either. But I didn't start thinking about how bad an idea it until after the stationery had been printed up and paid for. Now you know why the whole pile is still in my desk drawer.

I had a little black book filled with memories—don't all single women?—in which I'd carefully entered the names of the suspects, at least the female ones, along with their phone numbers and addresses. Somebody might have gone through it—maybe—but it was still in the drawer.

The desk pad! The desk pad was blank. But the top sheet should have held the impression of the notes I'd taken on how to get to Erica's apartment. You take a graphite pencil, like the one I took from my center drawer, run it lightly back and forth over the top of the pad, and voila you can see the marks of the preceding entry. Unless... someone has already pulled the trick with the pencil and taken the top sheet away.

So someone had broken into my office, gone through the desk drawers, and taken an impression of the desk pad. OK, someone could have. It could all be in my head, too. I walked over to the window and separated the blind with my finger and thumb. And someone could be out there sitting in one of the parked cars, watching the front door of my building just waiting for me to leave again.

But who? Couldn't have been Erica Mueller. I'd been talking to her when I made the notes. It couldn't have been Sara Newcombe, she'd have had to zip on several layers of clothes before she could dash down the back stairs after me. It might have been JoAnne Greene or any of the angry women who'd been at her place. This fitted with what I wanted to believe. Maybe the Manson-Greene family had decided individually or as a group that I was more dangerous than I looked. Or, it could have been someone else entirely, someone who'd talked with Marvin or JoAnne Greene after I left. When they learned I'd been to see Greene, they'd gotten very curious about who I was and how much I knew.

Not much, I can tell you. The interview with Erica had been pretty much of a bust. Oops, that's a bad pun. She denied her guilt and I believed her just as I had with JoAnne. I knew what I felt but I didn't know anything I could testify to in court. Or if I did know something, I didn't know I knew it.

Could be I was just being paranoid about the whole thing. Just because you're paranoid doesn't mean they're not out to get you.

I already said that, didn't I? Someone was out there watching. I checked the window blind again. I just hoped it wasn't the weird kid with all the mascara who was tailing me.She'd looked capable of all sorts of meanness.

I sat down at my desk and toyed with the desk pencil. (It was part of a set, but the pen was long gone). I doodled on the pad. I flipped the pencil in the air. I got up and looked out the window again.

Somebody? Nobody. Somebody was making a whooshing noise as they walked across the room. The hairs rose on the back of my neck and I wheeled angrily hands thrust forward in a defensive position. But the somebody was me. A 9x11 manila envelope was stuck to the sole of my shoe. I picked it up. To Phyllis Ludwisgson from the Five Star Talent Agency. It must have stuck to my shoe when I sat down at my desk. Five Star? That was Marvin.

The envelope might have contained an addendum to the list of suspects, an invitation to the agency ball, or the thirteenth volume of "My Philosophy" by Marvin the Agent. It might have held almost anything, once. Now, it was just an empty envelope.

Well, almost empty. Inside it, a studio photograph of Barbara taken full face still bore the imprint of my heel where I'd stepped on the envelope. And not just the imprint of my heel. Someone had written "bitch" over and over again on the envelope, until this word, too, had been impressed into the portrait's face.

I stared at the photo. Barbara had been a beautiful woman. I was glad her photographer had used color. He had captured the sunlight in Barbara's hair and the warmth that seemed to come from some inner fire. Her eyes were blue, no blue-gray. They looked back at me and seemed to read my thoughts, to care who I was and how I felt.

"You're beautiful," I said to the portrait. The portrait smiled. "Tell me what to do," I said aloud.

I stared at the photograph for a long, long time. Then I phoned Marvin.

"Did you send me anything this morning, Marvin?" I asked into the phone.

"Yeah," came the now familiar whining voice, "I dropped off a backgrounder on Barbara. That place of yours is a pigsty. How do you ever find anything?"

"You were in my office?" I choked.

"Sure. I figured since the door was open you were coming back soon, but your office is not exactly a place to wait, you know."

Now hold on Marvin, I live here. "How'd you get in my office?"

"Through the door."

"No, I mean. . ."

"It wasn't locked, if that's what you mean."

"It wasn't locked! What was in the envelope?"

"Are you drinking, Ludwigsohn? Little early in the day, don't you think?"

“Yes. No. I mean, I must have left the stuff on Barbara in the car.”

“Well, then go to your car. You’re going to need that stuff I gave you to help you on the case. Why do you think I brought it over?

“It’s mainly the standard press kit of course. Barbara’s college record. Her pro scores, amount of money she’s won. A couple of photographs. All the stuff on Barbara’s Kids.”

“What’s Barbara’s Kids?”

“You know, it was in all the papers. Like Jerry’s Kids. It was my idea. Barbara’s Kids is kind of a halfway house for orphans, the older ones, who can’t get adopted and can’t get along with their foster parents. Barbara would take two or three of the kids under her wing personally, see that they got clothes, take them shopping, get them tickets to the games. Great publicity.

“Barbara really was a wonderful girl. We won’t see her like again. Not for a long while. A lot of people inside and outside of volleyball are going to miss her. You should read over the stuff I gave you. There was a reason I sent it to you.”

“I’ll read it Marv.”

“O.K. Chow.”

“Chow, Marvin. Wait! What are the kid’s names? Maybe I should talk to them?”

“What would they know? Just read the stuff I gave you.”

“O.K. Marv.” I was going to read it, just as soon as I found it, along with

the person or persons who had removed it from my office.

Chapter 6

My office building has a super. He's a Basque; they brought him over here originally to herd sheep in Montana, but he didn't care for the cold. Who does? We needed to have a talk about who'd been in the building, whether they'd come to my floor, how long they'd been there. All this, or course, assumed that he'd been on duty doing the repairs he was supposed to do and not in the basement drinking.

When I got to the basement, he'd a bottle in his hand. This was a good sign. If he'd started drinking earlier, the bottle would have been already empty and he'd have been snoring away on his cot. The cot was mine once; I finally moved it to the basement because I'd rather he slept off his binges down there than in my office. I don't see him as much anymore but that is just as well as he has a terrible fondness for onions and garlic.

The odors of both along with the smell of cheap whiskey greeted me as I entered his room.

"How are you Ms. L?"

"O.K. and you?"

"Couldn't be better."

So we had the amenities out of the way. "You been up and about today?"

"For sure, fixed that damn drainpipe. You had a pretty girl visit you. I should have been inside to greet her. You weren't there you know."

I knew. "What did she look like?"

He used his hands to carve out a description. Obviously, my visitor's bust had been ample enough, not exactly your patrician type.

I should have listened more closely to what he said next. "She said hello to me. Funny accent, she must come from Catalan."

Right. As far as he was concerned, everybody but him and a bunch of weird-ass sheepherders had a funny accent.

I made several further spirited attempts to extract information from him but his own earlier attacks on the spirits proved insurmountable. In fact, it was only as I was leaving Joe's cramped basement living quarters that he called out, "Hey Ms. L., you want to see something." Yeah, a picture of this woman you say came by. But what he pulled out instead from beneath his cot, wrapped in a particularly loathsome shirt, was a photograph of Barbara Dahl.

"Where'd you get that? What the hell were you doing in my office?"

"No, no, Ms. L. I no take from your office, I . . ." He reached for the English word and began to cry instead. Somehow, I was persuaded he was telling the truth. Maybe, it was the garlic-laden belches that accompanied his denial. "I show you," he said, standing up, still not having found the phrase he was reaching for. He led me out the door and up the basement stairs. Led is not quite the operative word for he staggered rather than walked and I was forced to hold him up each time receiving only whiffs of half-digested onion and anchovies for my efforts. What we detectives won't do to crack a case.

We ended in front of the battered green dumpster at the side of the building. Still crying, he was only able to point to it. I raised the lid expecting the worst, but it was practically empty with only a few eight and a half by eleven pages of high-quality stationery lying on the stained bottom.

I pondered how best to retrieve them: tell Joe to step inside or go back upstairs, change my clothes and do it myself. I temporized, folding a newspaper I found lying nearby over the edge of the dumpster, then leaning in as far as I could. Page by page my efforts were rewarded with the missing press releases Marvin had spoken of.

"Joe, you're going to have to tell me more about the woman who was here."

I got the hand gestures a second time, this time from the seated position where Joe had positioned himself against the building wall. Between gestures he was holding his head in his hands and moaning. O.K., so I was being cruel; I needed information.

"You saw her put the papers in the dumpster?"

"No, no, I look."Looking for enough empty cans to buy another bottle of cheap liquor.

"What did the woman look like, Joe, like the girl in the picture?"

"No, she blond. She looks like me." He pointed to his own gray head, belched one last time and fell back against the wall asleep. I did what even a pig would do under the circumstances: got up and slowly walked away.

Chapter 7

But I didn't give up. Promising myself that I would get around, eventually, to reading the materials Marvin had sent me, I set out for my next interview. At this point in the investigation of Barbara Dahl's murder, my score was not an impressive one. I'd had interviews with two of the suspects, three if you count the portrait of a dead woman, and learned nothing of value. It could be argued that I've never really been very effective with women I found attractive and, alas, this was one case in which female suspects abounded.

Fortunately, at least one of the suspects, the redhead, Diane Purdy, appeared to be 100% normal (barring a perhaps not quite suppressed inclination to put strychnine in the water supply of those with whom she disagreed).

I'd spent a good part of my time at the tournament last Sunday afternoon gazing at Diane Purdy's freckled shoulders—she'd refereed the semifinal and final matches—and enjoying her smile. I'd also spent a good part of my time since developing and expanding on fantasies that involved her.

Purdy was pretty. So ran the least salacious of the thoughts that ran through my head early the next morning as I drove to Diane Purdy's house for an interview much like Rock Hudson (in his he-man days) had set out pursuing Doris Day.

I think it was Diane's devil-may-care attitude that inspired me. She made a hell of a referee. And with her combination of all-American girl grin and all-European body, she'd make a hell of a life partner. (Not that I wasn't almost committed in that direction; but you've got to preserve your options.)

It was hard to figure how a suburban housefrau—to use Erica's words—had made it onto Marvin's five-most-likely-suspects list, but there Diane was. Why argue when the gods are on your side? And interviewing Diane at home, sure beat trying to interview JoAnne Greene in the Manson family living room.

As Erica had predicted, Diane's home was a sweet little ranch house on the edge of suburbia. Fresh white paint with green trim, manicured lawn, flowers in clumps of blues and pinks, white border fence enclosing the back yard, and in the center, a magnificent orange tree loaded with fruit. A perfect match for Diane's wholesome good looks. I could see myself living in a cottage like this, working nine to five, and spending my evenings with Diane at meetings of the P.T.A. O.K., so a really good detective would have realized that a cottage made for two already had two in it, but I still had ten minutes worth of fantasy left to go.

The Diane who answered the door was everything I remembered and a little bit more, perky breasts, sparkling blue eyes, and reddish blond hair. Ever notice that a blouse and shorts can be ten times as sexy as a bikini, especially when the blouse is just a little bit smaller than it should be and one frayed button keeps working loose? If you could be tolerant of an over abundance of freckles, and a perhaps overly large Sally Kellerman mouth, then Diane probably would be the woman for you, too.

It was her smile that did it for me, a wild, I'm having a wonderful time, aren't you too smile.

"You're a hell of a referee," I said, just to start the conversational ball rolling.

"Damn right," she said, grinning from ear to ear.

"I'm here to ask you a few questions about Barbara."

"Damn right. That's the best line I've heard in a long time, isn't it dear?"

Her endearment startled me. From what little I could see of the house from the entryway, we were alone. Forget that "Dear!" On with the action plan. What would it be first, the interrogation or the sex? A tad more interrogation might be best; give it another five minutes before the two of us gave way to our mutual passion.

"O.K., so tell me all about Barbara Dahl."

"Barbara was a warm wonderful person. Everybody tried to get along with her. Some tried harder than others. She was a great beach volleyball player despite her age. Being 6'1" didn't hurt."

"How old is she, was she?"

"You don't know?"

I shook my head.

"Well, I'm not going to be the one to spoil your fantasies. C'mon in the living room. Want a beer?"

"No. Yes." Damn, was she laughing at me. I hadn't been staring too obviously at her mammaries had I? I mean I'm really more into legs.

"No. Yes? Shall I pour you half a beer?"

"Yes. No."

"Yes. No. No. Yes. You must wow all the girls. She's as smooth an operator as you, dear." This last remark was directed toward a mound of hirsute flesh that was propped before a computer terminal in one corner of the living room.

Diane ran her fingers through the mound's hair.

"I work at home," the mound said by way of explanation.

"Isn't he just the biggest teddy-bear," she said hugging it or him. Why, I asked myself, and not for the first time, did women like her always end up with guys like him? I bet I wasn't the first of Diane's admirers to ask that. I bet everyone she'd ever dated, everyone who'd ever wanted to date her had asked that. But that's the way it is folks. Not only was Diane Purdy married to a fat slob, but she was married to a fat slob who worked out of his home and would be ears at the ready throughout our entire interview. So much for the fantasies. (I probably wouldn't have made a pass at her anyway. Takes me a year sometimes to work up the courage to kiss a new partner. Well, maybe on the second date, if she's not as shy as I am.)

"Who did Barbara like? Who were her friends?" I asked just to be asking something different.

"Everybody," she said, "Except for niggers, n'spicks, n'jews..."

"n'catholics, n'presbyterians, n'men who wore gold chains," her husband put in from behind the computer terminal

." . . men who didn't know how to dress properly, women who didn't dress the same way she did."

"What my wife is trying to say is that Barbara was a bigoted, prejudiced no good bitch."

"Hey. I can say that. I don't need your help. Barbara was a bigoted, prejudice no good bitch."

"But you said everybody liked her."

"I said everybody got along with her. You had to get along with Barbara or you were out on your ass. She was one fierce dragon lady. And she had the power."

"Power? What do you mean by power? Being the champion gives you power?"

"You'd better believe it. If you are a winner like Barbara you get the most of everything—sponsors, court time, total control."

"Not that this worries you." her husband said proudly.

"Nothing worries me," Diane said. "I told her she was a stuck-up no-good bitch to her face, any number of times."

"My wife can tell people that and they take it." A large grin emerged from somewhere in the center of that mass of hair. Now I knew the guy could read my thoughts.

"Which makes Diane a prime suspect." I interjected.

"My wife! A killer?"

"Michael! You know I've got the killer instinct." she clowned. "Wow, this is exciting. I'm a murder suspect. Am I your only suspect?" she asked me.

"I've got five others. I'd kind of like your opinion on each one. But first tell me a little more about Barbara."

"Like what?"

"Like how she used her power for instance."

"How didn't she use it? She dictated our hair-do's, even our clothes. They said the T.V. people wanted it that way, but we knew it was Barbara."

"She chose your clothes?"

"Call them uniforms if you like. She'd been doing it since high school. I could tell you a story. . ." Diane stopped and looked around the room. This time she blushed. "What am I afraid for?" she mumbled under her breath, stopped again, and then went on in a normal voice which grew faster and shriller as she spoke: "When Barbara was a senior, she was on some sort of committee that got to chose the color of the court shoes and knee socks for the following year. When the shoes show up, half of them are white with yellow stripes and half are yellow with white stripes. Barbara goes through the roof, and the parent's committee—and you've got to remember this is high school and all the equipment is being paid for by the parents and not by the school—the committee sends them back. They buy all the shoes locally, pay twice as much for them, but Barbara's happy. Get this, every kid now has to pay for her own shoes. If you were poor, you or your parents had to pay for them, whether or not they really had the money."

"You were poor," I said.

"I was poor."

"Look um, were there some maybe positive things that Barbara did?"

"I don't want to talk about her."

"You know positive stuff like Barbara's Kids. Didn't she adopt some kids?"

"What kids!!"

"Maybe, you could like change the subject." Diane's husband interrupted.

"Oh yeah, yeah sure." Something was very wrong. I liked Diane, but I liked, had liked Barbara also. Joe the superintendent wasn't the only one keeping a copy of her picture near him. But some of the things I was learning about her were disturbing if, that is, I chose to believe what I was hearing. I was sorry Barbara and Diane had not got along. But it was just too late to do anything about it.

"Could I maybe ask you a few questions about some of the other suspects?"

"Fire away." Diane replied, starting to get back her smile.

"Like I said, I've got a list of five uh four suspects. The first is, uh, Derek Chzynski."

"Mama's boy. He'd only kill someone if his mother told him to. I suggest you check into mama."

"Mama's boy?" said Diane's husband, "He's got muscles on his muscles."

"Mama's boy. Don't argue with me. I know a real man when I see one."

Her husband blushed; at least he may have blushed somewhere under all that hair.

"Erica Mueller."

"Why would she bother? She's got Sara, now."

"She's got ... Are you telling me that Sara? And that Barbara and Sara?"

"Look dear," she said to her husband, "she's back to being embarrassed again. Can't even finish her sentences.

"Do I turn you on that much?" she said to me with a look.

"Yes you do." I took a deep breath, dropped my voice an octave, and did my very best to imitate a tough cop. "Now let's have it straight. You say that Sara Newcombe and Erica Mueller are having an affair. And that Sara Newcombe and Barbara Dahl used to be having an affair."

"Yeah. Doesn't it just bum you out. Sweet little Sara with that bitch Erica. I bet you had twice as much eyes for her as you had for me."

I had, I had, but I'd also had eyes for that bitch Erica. Back to the tough cop, "How do you explain Barbara's engagement to Derek?"

"Window dressing. I told you he was a mama's boy."

"Sara Newcombe."

"Never. She led Barbara by the nose. She was the only one who could."

"Chara DeCastro."

"You're kidding! Chara?"

"Her name was on the list." (Or at least JoAnne Greene had put it there.)

"Chara can't even speak English for Christ's sake, how's she going to go around buying poison? Did you hear her at the tournament, she says 'dig' and she means 'set.' Besides, with Barbara as her partner she'd have made fifty grand this summer."

"I heard you giving her an English lesson."

"I give all kinds of lessons." This last was accompanied by a wink and tit toss that was straight out of Tom Jones. Somehow with her husband only ten feet away I figured it was just another put on. Hah, I knew it was a put on. It was, wasn't it?

"Dee-Dee Williams." said Diane's husband.

"What!" said Diane.

"She's not on the list," I said.

"Barbara hated blacks. Ergo, blacks hated her. Q.E.D." said Diane's husband.

"Be real," said Diane. "Besides, Dee-Dee doesn't even play beach ball. Who else is on the list?"

"Well, there's you," I said to her.

"Out of the question," said her husband.

Diane turned to him with a fierce expression that got still fiercer as she spoke. "I already told you. I can kill as easily as the next girl. Stop putting me down."

"Ah," continued her husband logically, ignoring the intensity of her remarks, "but you are a crack rifle shot. You'd have got her with your rifle while she was jogging on the beach."

I tended to agree. Most people who kill take the path of least resistance. But then most people who kill also get caught and put away.

"True." Diane said, smiling again, "The hit was on for Monday. Just my luck some other slut got to her first."

"What about your volleyball partner, Lana ... Lana something?" I asked.

"Lana Wilms. Impossible. Too laid back. You might as well accuse JoAnne Greene."

"Why not JoAnne Greene?" her husband interjected, "JoAnne was doing awfully well on the circuit before Barbara came along."

"Why not me? I was always good for another round in the tournament before Barbara. What you're forgetting is that once Barbara came along we all got more money. I make more for eighth place now than I used to for first."

"True," said the hairy one, "Barbara was what the game needed to get into the big TV money. Someone irresistible and sexy."

"You bastard," Diane said, leaping at him, "That's me." While her first few blows must have really hurt, the attack soon degenerated into a lot of pawing and groping and some truly disgusting kissing sounds. No question about it. Purdy was pretty. But she already had her Teddy bear.

"What about fixing Ms. Detective up with Clarice?" her husband asked when he came up for air.

Diane looked me carefully up and down. She didn't exactly devour me with her eyes the way she had in my fantasies, but it was a pleasant enough experience. I imagine strippers feel the same way.

"Naaah. She's too laid back. They'd never make contact."

So much for that fragment of a dream.

Chapter 8

The view from Diane's porch was of a series of terraces gradually rising into the green foothills of the nearby mountains. The morning sun had painted the boulders in red and orange and ochre.

Diane's husband came out on the porch with a beer in each hand.

"Mike Purdy," he said handing me one.

"Phyllis Ludwigsohn," I replied. Mike was a big man, a lot bigger and a lot taller than he'd seemed in his chair. If you saw him on the street with his scraggly beard and unkempt hair, you'd probably think he drank Gallo and ate out of dumpsters, but this close you could see the intelligence shining from his eyes.

"It may be too early for a beer," he said diffidently, but his voice was hopeful.

"Not at all," I said gratefully. The first sip was wonderful. So were sips two and three.

"Your home is beautiful," I said, "And this canyon! God. It seems just perfect for the two of you."

"It's a long way from the beach," he said.

"Yeah, but look what you get in its place." I waved my arms inarticulately at the well-cared lawn and garden, and the other well-cared lawns and gardens nearby, and the great granite boulders, and the green foothills that merged with the faraway blue sky.

"Diane would like to be closer to the beach, but it's all we can afford."

I thought of what I could afford, a tiny apartment in a mixed ethnic neighborhood, a one-room office near the docks. "You're doing O.K."

"Thanks." He grinned. His grin had the same infectious quality his wife's grin had. "Yeah, it is nice. But I feel bad sometimes because it is so far from the beach. Diane says she doesn't mind, but..."

He paused and looked at me expectantly. I wasn't sure what he wanted me to say and said nothing. Let him speak. Let him say what he'd come out on the porch to tell me.

"You know, I helped her perfect her technique. We make films of her games and then analyze all her moves. I use the computer. It's one of the ways she's been able to keep up in the pros despite her height.

"She's got a lot of heart, also."

"God yes," he replied fervently.

We were silent again. I was down to the last drops of my beer. And he still hadn't said what he'd come out on the porch to tell me. How was I going to put it into words for him, you love your wife very much, but you think she's a killer.

He broke the silence first.

"I was hoping I might be able to help you," he said.

My mouth opened then closed without a word coming out. He'd not said what I expected him to say.

"I thought maybe, you know, I would be able to help you to sift through clues and track down the murder."

I gave him a look. This was a new one on me, a suspect, or rather a suspect's husband who said he wanted to help.

"There a lot you can do with computers, today: matching identifications, double-checking schedules. One suspect says she was on the beach at eleven. Another suspect says no, she was at the grocery store."

I took another swig of my beer. "There's not much logic in this case," I replied, "it seems to be all raw emotion."

"Do you have a time table for each suspect?"

I'm lucky if I can just get people to talk to me, I thought irreverently. "I'm not at that stage yet, I mean, I'm not even sure where I'd want the suspects to be."

"Ah, but you could still check their statements to see if anyone is lying, you could look for contradictions."

"I could if I had tape recordings or notes we could go over."

"You don't have notes?!"

"That's not the way I work. Look, I appreciate the beer. I appreciate the offer of help. But that's not why you came out to talk to me."

"The offer is genuine."

"I'm sure it is."

Again there was silence. The colors were disappearing now as the sun rose higher in the sky, but the impression of a vast open space was just as awe-inspiring.

He spoke finally. "You know, I just don't know where she is half the time."

"You mean Diane hasn't been coming home?" I said, surprised.

"No, nothing like that. I mean she'll sit staring into space, her mind a million miles away. 'What are you thinking about,' I'll ask. She doesn't even hear me."

"How long has this been going on?"

"Not long."

"When Barbara was still alive?"

He thought about it for a moment. "No. After. After she was..."

"Diane's probably been thinking about her own death. Or at least the possibility. I've been there myself. Why are we here? Are we doing what we should be doing? What will it be like when we die?"

He thought over what I'd said for a moment and then nodded his head in agreement.

"Is she moody?" I asked.

"Oh God. She's always moody."

Again I waited for him to speak, to say what he'd come out on the porch to say. Or maybe he had. Maybe a guy as happy as he was in his marriage just wanted his wife to be happy, too.

"I wonder who else was on that High School team," I said aloud.

"Or who wasn't."

He was full of surprises.

He went on, "Here's why I'm asking. We could get a list of the people on that team easy enough. A day or two and we could probably come up with a list of the people on Barbara's other teams and run them through the computer. But remember, Barbara had the power. This meant she could keep people off the court. These are the people I would worry about."

I thanked him, but I wasn't grateful. Now, I had twice as many suspects to worry about. That's the trouble with bringing other people in on a case. They come up with questions you haven't even thought of asking.

Chapter 9

Six suspects, three interviews. I was halfway through. Next on the list was Chara deCastro, Barbara Dahl's partner in that final game, and a recent addition to the lists of suspects, courtesy of JoAnne Greene. Chara had had the opportunity all right, but as Diane Purdy said it was hard to figure the motive. Chara's partnership with Barbara had almost guaranteed her big money for the rest of the season.

Chara did not seem to have a home in the classic sense; at least not one with an address and a phone number. Rumor had it that she needed to avoid the immigration authorities. But those in the know also said that Chara could be guaranteed to spend at least part of each day on the beach, and it was to the beach I headed.

As predicted, Chara was there on the sand in residence midway between the surf and the line of beach houses under a shelter formed from two beach umbrellas. Despite the casual nature of the candy-striped green and red parasols, her shelter had an air of permanence about it with clothes, shoes, cosmetics, towels, and even a portable hair dryer stacked neatly underneath. The day was not one of your all-time winners. The sky was overcast and apart from Chara's umbrellas the beach was virtually deserted. A cold stiff wind blowing in from the sea didn't help any. Obviously, the tourists had headed inland for Disneyland and Knott's Berry Farm. The beach regulars were all in Maui or, much to the surprise of their employers, at work.

Despite the cold, Chara was dressed in a makeshift bikini that revealed even more than the one she had worn on the day of the match. And despite the absence of sun, she was rubbing tanning oil into her dark satin skin. She smiled when she saw me, white even teeth, and called out what sounded to me like "Chiao." Although her dark skin was already glistening, she handed me the tanning oil. "Chiao?" she said again.

Assuming that "Chiao" meant "put the sun tan lotion on" in Spanish or Catalan, I said something like "sure" in return and bent to my task. Tentatively at first and then enthusiastically, as I sensed her movements.

"You have a beautiful body," I said. A whole series of unpronounceable words issued forth from Chara in reply. Something about my clothes. Too large, too much, something like that. "The day is cold." I said. Cold enough that I was actually wearing an old sweater over my slacks. One yank from Chara's powerful hands and I was nude to the waist. A second yank and I was in my panties. What's going on here?

Chara stopped undressing me at this point thankfully and lay back on her beach towel indicating that now, appropriately attired, I was ready to begin again.

Ever make love to a tiger? I mean did you ever run your fingers over the smooth sleek skin of a very powerful cat? Chara was like that. Muscular, but very, very feminine. And she purred like a cat whenever I bore down on one or the other part of her smooth feminine body.

After twenty minutes, I had finished her back, legs and arms included, and sank back on my haunches exhausted, but satisfied, if you know what I mean. She wasn't. She turned over on her back, undid the cloth strip she used for a halter, flicked it away and looked up at me. "Chiao?"

"Chiao!"

Her bottoms went too and then my skivvies were gone. She was on top of me and my bottom was grinding into the sand. Somehow we had rolled off the beach towel. My God, didn't she realize this was a public beach? I tried to roll free, but was given no opportunity. It is. . . it was rape. Someone, anyone help! Do you know how much sand you get in your crotch when you're on the bottom in a beach orgy?

"Chiao," Chara said as she sat up and readjusted her halter. My panties were just so much waste cotton and I put on my slacks directly over my bare and sandy bottom. "Chiao," Chara said again and bestowed a final sandy kiss on the spot where her mouth and tongue had been a moment before.

I laid my head on her breast, smelt her moistness, tasted again the mixture of lotion and salt that was uniquely hers, rested and heard in return the deep even breathing of the trained athlete. After awhile, I sat up and looked out at the ocean. A ship's mast could be seen far out on the horizon. A pelican flew over our heads, wingtips barely moving, in a long sustained circle that ended abruptly when it dived after a leaping fish. When I looked back at the blanket, Chara's eyes were closed. She was smiling, a broad satisfied smile, like a sleeping child caught in a dream. Could this be the face of a cold-blooded killer? I thought not.

As I walked to my car, I reflected on the interview and its merging of two cultures. The final score, Chara 1, Detective 1. With all costs borne by the Five Star Talent Agency. I still wasn't quite sure why she had chosen me, though I meant to look in the mirror at the first opportunity. And I made a mental note to pick up a bottle of tanning oil at the supermarket and carry it with me wherever I went. You never know when your services may be needed on the beach.

There was a second car in the parking lot, at the far end away from the entrance to the beach. It had not been there when I arrived. The sun, what there was of it, reflected off its windshield and I couldn't be sure if anyone was inside car. I got my binoculars out of the glove compartment and tried to make out the license number. No luck. The front bumper was facing me and all it had to say was, “Bill Neale’s Kansas City Chrysler-Plymouth.”

I started across the parking lot, notebook in hand, and stopped about thirty feet away. I still couldn’t see if anybody was inside. Maybe they were, maybe they weren’t. There sure as hell wasn’t anybody beside me walking around.

I had begun circling toward the rear, when the car started up suddenly and came racing toward me across the parking lot. It didn’t look friendly. I tossed my notebook to the side and started running, crisscrossing from side to side to make things tough for the following car. It swerved after me, the angel on the hood tracking me unerringly as a gun sight. Jesus, what if they had a gun!

I cut out the broken field running and headed back on the dead run for the beach, the big gray car directly on my tail. I leaped the concrete divider, flew over an old drift wood log and landed in the sand among the shards of Styrofoam and half-eaten burgers that had almost made it into the nearby trashcan. I was alive.

The car behind me gunned swiftly into reverse, turned and was out the entrance to the parking lot long before I could think to read the license number.

Chapter 10

A host of natural hazards make the boardwalk at Muscle Beach as dangerous as a freeway. The roller skaters come equipped with kneepads, ankle guards, and crash helmets to protect them in case of accident. The oldsters have lethal free-swinging canes and slow-moving walkers that pin you against the rail. But the rest of us pedestrians are strictly on our own.

Derek Chzynski was not on time for our appointment. Whoever was following me was; I'd have felt odd if they weren't. I gave Derek fifteen minutes on the clock and then went into the health club to look for him. I had a lot of places in which to look. What had once been a simple haven for weight lifters was now cluttered with Nautilus machines, a snack bar, a 1/8th mile track, and a Natatorium—the last a fancy name for a swimming pool. Plenty of mirrors, of course. Why build yourself up if you don't have an appreciative audience. After several misunderstandings and apologies, I found Derek on the far wall of the mirrored salon, one of a dozen other muscle-bound clones pitting his strength against a metal and chrome machine.

Derek wasn't exactly rude, but he wasn't apologetic either. "Sorry, I must have lost track of time. You wanted to ask me some questions?"

"Not here." I waited while Derek did six more quick lifts and then turned himself right side up. I waited while he showered and dressed, waited while he ordered something quick and dreadful from the health club snack bar in the way of a carrot juice and tigers milk smoothie. And I waited till he'd drained the shake in a single gulp and stepped outside. Then I put it to him.

"A couple of witnesses say your engagement to Barbara was strictly window dressing."

Fast footwork beats muscles every day. Ask anyone who was watching when he swung on me. A quick Aikido move, the one and only Aikido move I know, and his punch whistled harmlessly by. I thought of putting his arm in a come-along hold behind his back, but why add insult to injury? Besides, I was physically drained from that morning on the beach.

Derek looked drained, emotionally anyway. He still had muscles on his muscles. "Look, I loved Barbara and she loved me. It was a normal engagement in every way. I don't know what somebody else may have told you, but Barbara was a real woman.

"Sure she'd made it with women, but she was through with that. And I'm the one who showed her the way."

I stared at him for one full moment and then said, "Uh huh." I'd learned a lot from my brother's ex-wife.

"Look. Barbara changed, we changed together. I don't know who told you the stories, but they're not true. Barbara and I were lovers. Would I lie about something like that?"

Answer: Yes, and yes.

"Look." he shouted at me so that a pair of roller skaters looked up as they elbowed by, "Go talk to Barbara's mother. Talk to her brothers. They'll tell you how real our engagement was.

"We'd even planned our family. We were going to adopt. Two of Barbara's Kids. A girl for her and a boy for me. Greg was his name."

"How nice for you." I replied. "Maybe it was a real engagement. And maybe one day after Barbara had sworn love and eternal fidelity, you found her back in bed with a chick, Sara Newcombe maybe. And you killed Barbara, killed her because you couldn't take the blow to your pride."

"No, you've got it all wrong. I loved Barbara and she loved me. If there's anyone with a motive, it would be Sara. She's the one who was rejected."

Not the way I'd heard it. But I kept my thoughts to myself; I learn more by asking questions. "So, you think Sara murdered Barbara?"

"I didn't say that."

"Then who was the killer? Erica? JoAnne Greene?"

"It might have been."

"JoAnne, Erica? Which one?"

"JoAnne Greene."

"Why?"

"They . . . they both wanted to be in charge."

"They both wanted to be in charge? That's it?"

"Look. Barbara used to play for JoAnne. And JoAnne . . . JoAnne's the one who got her started with women. You understand?"

I just looked at him. After awhile, he looked away. When he began to talk again, his hand was over his mouth as if he were trying to recapture his words as fast as he said them.

"Barbara was an awfully mixed up kid once. And JoAnne's just the sort of person to take advantage. She tries it on with all her players. Maybe JoAnne just flipped out when she found that Barbara really preferred men."

It was a possibility. It was also the second possibility that Derek had handed me in the last two minutes. If I kept him talking long enough, I was sure he'd try to pin motives on the other three suspects.

"You say that Barbara used to be an awfully mixed up kid?"

"It was Barbara's family of course. You've talked with her family. You know what they're like."

Oops. Actually, I had not talked with Barbara's family. Big dummy that I am, I'd faithfully gone down the list of suspects Marvin had handed me without doing what any Keystone Cop would have down at the start. But I wasn't going to admit all this to Mr. Muscles.

"I suppose her family knew all about you and Barbara."

"Yes. I mean no, not everything. I mean they didn't know Barbara and I had been sleeping together. It's not the sort of thing you talk about with your mother. They knew we were going to be married. And they knew we'd talked about adopting."

"Had you set the wedding date?"

He didn't say anything. For a moment, I thought he was going to cry. All the more reason to press on ahead. "I suppose you're also the only one who can give you an alibi at the time of the murder."

"I was at the Iron Man meet."

"What?"

"Lackland's Iron Man competition. They hold it every year at the same time they hold the women's volleyball tournament. That's why I wasn't at the finals to see Barbara. That's why I didn't get there . . . ."

And he broke off, sobbing, his hands covering his face, real tears, I think.

Of course, Derek hadn't been at the match. He'd been in the Iron Man Triathlon they were holding at the same time. And the finals of the volleyball tournament had taken place while he was still competing, I remembered. I'd been on the beach watching the start of the triathlon, and I'd been at the volleyball court after Barbara's death when he'd come running up still dripping from the surf. But had I seen Derek in the Iron Man lineup?

It was hard to be sure. I might have seen him. I might not have. Hell, I hadn't recognized him when I was in the gym; I'd had to ask somebody. Even now in his blue striped shirt and white shorts, he looked like a dozen other guys, muscular ones to be sure.

I wasn't going to be his alibi.

But he'd come in fourth in the triathlon. In fact, he'd come close to winning the competition—he'd blown it in the final leg, pooping out on the surfboard, in front of two hundred onlookers. Now there was an alibi. But could the people watching on the beach really be sure it was Derek they were watching far out in the water? Couldn't somebody else have worn his number?

Naah. He had too many witnesses. Derek had to have been on the beach. And if Derek was in the Iron Man competition at 4 p.m. then he wasn't at the volleyball tournament when Barbara was poisoned. He couldn't have killed his girlfriend. Or if he had, leaving poison in one of the half-dozen water bottles in the hopes that Barbara would drink it, it would be at the risk of killing a dozen other people instead. Not. As of now, I couldn't pin the murder on Derek any more than I could on Sara or Erica or the other fifty suspects the police had on tape.

Suddenly, the hairs on the back of my neck stood on end. I took a slow look around the boardwalk. O.K. whoever you are hiding in the shadows, I know you're watching me.

"What is it?" Derek asked.

"Just thought I recognized somebody."

"Look if you're all through asking questions, I'd like to...";

he stopped.

"I'm all through," I said.

"Look if you find the person who... If you need help or anything, you..."

He couldn't finish his sentences, but I knew what he meant. "Thanks," I said.

"You'll find them," he said, but he was really asking a question.

"I'll find them."

He walked one way on the boardwalk. I walked the other. I'd find Barbara's killer, maybe. There were a few more leads I could follow. Barbara's Kids, for one. Was it real or all for show? I should check out Dee-Dee Williams. And I would check out Barbara's family as I should have on day one of the investigation. Derek had given me their address. But first, I had a date with an angel.

Chapter 11

The next name on my list was that of Sara Newcombe, volleyball's number one pinup, at least, now that Barbara Dahl was gone. I knew there was no way, no way, I would get an interview with Sara at Chez Mueller, her current abode. But we private detectives have our ways. According to the brief bio that Marvin the advance man had assembled for me, Sara was either taking or teaching a course at the local J.C. this summer, and it was to Marina Junior College that I went in search of my last and loveliest suspect.

Through sheer dumb luck, I found Sara sitting outside the administration building, eating her lunch from a paper sack. She was wearing a straight cotton skirt with no belt, and a white T-shirt with a beach volleyball graphic on it in peach and black and green. Even fully clothed she was outstanding, and I could tell that the five young males in her near vicinity hadn't just located themselves there accidentally.

She seemed oblivious to them, however, and, for a while, even to me, though I was sitting next to her breathing heavily.

"Good afternoon, Ms. Lewisohn isn't it," she said in a soft, husky voice not much louder than the wind in the nearby palm trees.

"Ludwigsohn," I corrected absent-mindedly.

"How about if I call you Phyll."

"Sure," I smiled.

She smiled back. Let me tell you something; there was just no way, no way a woman with a smile like this could be sharing a bed with Erica Mueller, could be Barbara Dahl's former lover, could have been seduced by JoAnne Greene. But, of course, I knew better.

"Erica didn't kill Barbara," Sara said, beating me to the punch, "She didn't need to."

"Because she had you," I replied, equally quick off the mark.

"Right." To give Sara credit, she blushed, but the dash of rose on her peach colored skin only served to further arouse the half dozen males who sat near by. Several literally twisted in agony. If only they knew what I knew. "I didn't kill Barbara either," she said.

She pulled a huge clasp knife from her paper bag. She opened the knife slowly and ran the blade along the edge of one slim finger. With several pairs of male eyes following her every move, she wiped the side of the blade with her napkin. She reached into the bag again and took out a large navel orange. Holding the orange in one hand, she inserted the knife a nail's width at the top. Three quick flicks of her wrist and she had cut a spiral slash around and down the orange. She removed the skin almost effortlessly and then proceeded to break the orange into sections.

"Would you like a piece?" she asked.

"Sure," I said. And stuck the section in my mouth.

"You know how you can tell I didn't kill her?" she said after a moment.

"You would have used a knife."

"I did use a knife at the end when Barbara wouldn't take no for an answer. I'm very good with a knife."

"I don't remember any knife marks on her body."

"They wouldn't have been visible to most people."

I thought for a moment about the bikini Barbara had been wearing the day she died. "They must have been very intimate knife wounds." I said.

"They were."

We sat in silence. A few students sauntered by on their way to the next class. It was plain that Sara's male admirers had taken to wondering about me the way I had marveled over Diane Purdy's husband. Beauty and the beast. Just didn't figure, did it? Well, eat your heart out boys.

Sara spoke finally. Her mood had changed. She was more reflective almost sad.

"She really wasn't a very nice person."

"Barbara?" I said, incredulously.

"At first, it was something very special. I'd known her for a long, long time before we... Did you know that I'd known her before?"

"No, I . . ."

"She was the star in high school, when I was just a freshman. And then when I started college, she was the star again."

"You didn't speak much, eh."

"Are you kidding? Seniors don't have much time for freshmen. They look right through you as if you weren't there. I made the team though. I got to fetch balls for the starters and take down and put up the net. We won the championship that year. It was great for the team but it also meant I never got off the bench."

"You were a star in high school though. That's what someone told me."

"Not a star. But I was a good player. I made the first team my sophomore year. Both times, high school and college. And both times, Barbara had gone on and wasn't there to see me. Sort of like an older sibling whom you just can't seem to impress.

"Then after college, when JoAnne asked me to play for her club team, there was Barbara again."

"And that's when you got to know her?"

"No. Yes. Not at first. I was still shy. Yes, I was shy. Believe me."

I looked at her. Clear skin, perfect features like something out of a photograph. "O.K. If you say so."

"Honest. I'm shy. Maybe that's why I never did date boys. If JoAnne hadn't pushed, I never really would have met Barbara."

"JoAnne wanted you to ...?

"JoAnne wanted it to be the way it had been when I played for her in college. And I told her it was all over. I'd changed. She'd changed too.

"I just wanted someone who would let me be me. With JoAnne, I would always be that fresh little girl she'd picked off the bench.

"And, of course, JoAnne and Barbara were always quarreling."

"JoAnne and Barbara quarreled?"

"About everything. They were both used to being in charge. They would fight in front of the team. The least little thing. That's why Barbara quit to play beach ball full time. And I quit to go with her."

"I understand."

"I think you do. Thank you for listening." She smiled again, that same wonderful radiant smile. I waited to hear what she would say or do next. All of us sitting near her waited and hoped the school bell wouldn't interrupt, the next class wouldn't take her away.

She looked down at her watch. It was one p.m. or close to it. "Look. I've got to go. I want to talk to you. But I've got to go."

"I do have more questions." I said.

"I have a faculty meeting now and I have to teach a class at two. We could meet at three."

"Here?"

“I’ll be down at the women’s gym. Do you know where it is?”

“I’ll find it.”

Sara smiled. She put the orange peels carefully into the paper bag, crumpled it and tossed it carelessly into a nearby litter basket. Then she walked off across the campus, hips swaying, long hair blowing carelessly into the wind. Her chorus of male admirers died a thousand deaths. So did I.

Chapter 12

I waited in the sun for a half an hour or so, watching the students at play. Their courtship rituals were as complicated as those of any mating bird. The girl shifted back and forth on one leg, holding out an armload of books for balance as she listened, the boy puffed out his chest and elevated his shoulders. When the watching palled, and the students themselves drifted away, I strolled across campus in the direction of the gym.

Marina has a small but scenic campus. Most of the buildings have been thrown up in the past seven or eight years, at least they looked part of that new style which is all rough-hewed stone and tinted glass. The central area of the campus is a sloping lawn, with a glimpse of the ocean far off in the distance. I made my way slowly down the steep path, but occasionally a student would come bounding by like some sort of mountain goat. I imagined if I had classes on opposite ends of that campus, I'd be bounding back and forth like a mountain goat, too. Fortunately, I could take my time, admire the palm trees, the rock gardens, and the sunlight reflected from the sea below.

The architect had done a very clever job disguising the gym. From the outside it looked like any of the other stone campus buildings. In fact, a false facade facing the lawn made it look as if it were two short buildings instead of one rather long one. Only the absence of windows on the first floor gave it away, that and the clumps of students in the doorways with sports bags and squash rackets in their hands.

A college campus may have its own unique atmosphere, but the insides of gymnasiums are all the same. They may not look the same, in some the basketball court is stretched lengthwise, in others it runs across the gym, but they smell and sound the same, the timeless odor of stale sweat, bouncing balls, screeching voices, and squeaking Reeboks, partially muffled by a cavernous interior. I wonder if there is a scent they spray the walls with before they dedicate a new gym. Probably.

The woman's gym at Marina J.C. held a bevy of young females at work having fun. A cluster of coeds, mostly African-American, were down at one end under the hoops. In the far corner, four girls were watching one another take turns on the mat and another set of four were grouped around the balance beam. Down at my end of the gym a dozen or more girls, part of a class, stood in a circle passing a volleyball back and forth under the watchful eye of a harried female instructor, not Sara, alas. What the students lacked in ability, they made up in noise, a constant stream of chatter unrelated to the tasks at hand. I smiled sympathetically at the instructor, a spare looking female with muscular arms and legs, but got only a scowl in reply.

The seven girls in the court next to me were more professional—I'd like to have that kind of light touch on my passes, but they were every bit as noisy. They were kind of hard looking, too, almost mannish, not the sort of girls I'd want to take home to my mother, though one of them, a tall fulsome blond wearing light blue knee socks, would be considered attractive in any group. When I picked up a ball that had rolled to my feet, the blond was the one who took the ball from me.

"Thanks pretty lady." Yes, it was me she was calling to. While a smile from her wasn't a smile from Sara, it made up for some of the rejections of the past week.

"Hi. You're fairly attractive, too," I said.

"You look a lot better than you did a couple of days ago." the blond persisted. "That tweaky jacket and those shoes you wore. Where do you get clothes like that, East Germany? Now you look normal. Doesn't she look normal, Deb."

"No, she still looks like a dope," Deb, an angular brunette, replied. Wait, I recognized this one. Put mascara around and under Deb's eyes and crayola around her lips and you had the cretin from JoAnne's apartment. This meant the blond was one of the Manson Family, too. Maybe all seven of them were.

"Deborah. Behave." the blond said. "Hey, you want to play with us? We're short a couple of guys." When I looked hesitant, she added, "you'll do fine."

I'd do better than fine. Little did they know I'd been playing pickup ball at the Y for almost three years now. And we play rough.

I tried not to let my enthusiasm show. "I'm not dressed for it," I said.

"You've got running shoes. And you could take off your blouse. Unless, you're embarrassed."

"She's wearing jeans," Deborah said practically.

"She could play in her skivvies." said the blond. Again she gave me her radiant smile.

"Thanks, I'll just take off my shirt." There was a rush of names as we lined up, "Leah, and Deborah, and Lou, and Potzie." Potzie was the blond girl. Potzie was lined up beside me. Deb or Deborah, thankfully, was on the other side of the net.

I'd have liked to warm up with the group, volley a few times, practice my serve, but apparently they'd just been waiting for even teams to get started. The other team, Deborah's, had the serve. I'd just as soon have been up by the net where my height would have done me some good, but instead I was back in the hot spot in the center of my team's back row waiting for the serve.

They don't call it the hot spot for nothing. Seventy percent of the defensive plays start right here. I shifted my weight from side to side a couple of times, and flexed my ankles. Pretty stiff; I wished I'd had time to warm up; it would be another half hour or so before I would be loose enough.

The serve came in hard and fast on my right, far enough away from me that I could feel relieved and not guilty when Potzie took the serve and passed it up the net. A good pass, a good set, and a good spike, side out for our side. I smiled at Potzie as she went back to serve; she smiled back at me.

Potzie's serve wasn't much of a challenge for the other team, and the return came down hard and fast a few inches from my face. Lou, on my left, charged in hard and fast and the two of us collided. I hit the deck, rolled, and was up on my feet in time to receive the ball smack in my face.

"Are you O.K.?" Potzie asked.

"I'm O.K." I said, though my eyes were tearing. There was a haze over my vision and I wanted to rub my nose so bad. Up at the net, Deborah laughed, a short harsh bark. No question who had hit that ball at me.

It was their serve again and again the ball came in hard and fast on my right, though this time it broke at the last moment and headed straight for me. My ball. At the edges of my still blurred vision, I could see Lou and Potzie coming in fast from either side, like two defensemen about to put the boots to Wayne Gretsky. But it's my ball, I thought inanely.

Bam! Just like in the comic books.

I was down. Lou stepped on me. Potzie's shoe collided with my skull, accidentally I hoped, and trying to scramble out of the way she kicked me in the nose a second time. But the ball was still in play. Across the net, Deborah went up in the air for a decisive smash. My blockers stepped out of the way! The ball came down straight and hard for my face without anyone to block it, eighty-five miles an hour. I grabbed my knees with my hands, pulled into a ball, and tried to roll out of the way.

Wham again! Right in the small of my back. I lay still on the gymnasium floor hoping that things would get better. There wasn't a muscle in my body that hadn't been bruised or beaten on that play. And the laughter, the loud raucous laughter was worse than any of the bruises.

Silence. I looked up through the haze and saw Sara Newcombe looking down on me. She reached out her hand. I grabbed it and she pulled me up on my feet. I took a step, still a little unsteady, and looked around. The entire Manson family was standing there looking back at me, grinning. And Potzie's grin was the widest of all.

Sara gave Potzie a look that would have withered oranges, then led me off the court, striding like a mother who has just rescued her kid from a gang of bullies. I could hear the laughter behind me, but Sara didn't stop until we were out of the gym. "Put on your blouse," she said.

I put on my shirt and tucked it in my jeans. "Looks better out," she said, "and roll down your pant legs." I rolled them down and started to tuck in my shirt again. "Let me do it," she said. "There, you look better.

"You're a good sport." She kissed my nose. "That's just a friendship kiss," she said before I could say anything.

"Thanks friend," I said.

We strolled up the hill. I thought of taking her hand, then thought better of it. In China maybe I'd have done it, or some other place where holding hands just meant you're friends.

We walked to a clump of rocks that had a view of the ocean. Sara pulled herself up neatly, and I scrambled along behind. The view was beautiful. So was Sara.

A couple of strolling males sat down on the lawn so they could look up at Sara's legs while they pretended to talk. To hell with them.

I launched into my speech. "Look Sara, I appreciate your help. I've got a job to do and I'm not sure I'm really doing it very well. There's a list of people who we think might have killed Barbara and I'd like to go over that list with you."

"Sure." With the "sure," came the smile and a slight movement of her body. The two male students, on their feet again, walked into a tree.

"Erica Mueller is the obvious suspect."

"I've already told you about her. She's a really fine, very emotional, very honest person. She's also very responsible."

"What about Chara DeCastro, or Derek, or some of the other people Barbara knew?"

"Chara's too inside herself. Kind of a space cadet, you know. She likes volleyball, she likes her body, she likes to sit on the beach."

"Were she and Barbara?"

Sara shrugged her shoulders. Her male audience, swollen in numbers, panted audibly. "Maybe."

"Derek?"

"Be real." She pouted, showing off all her dimples. "I don't think Derek's ever made it with anybody. It's all tanning lotion and body grease with him. Frankly, I don't think he likes girls. He never looked at me."

That was the clincher in my book.

I ran my eyes over Sara's body, why should the students have all the fun? But Sara was a million million miles away.

"She just wasn't the same," Sara said finally.

"Barbara?" I questioned, but Sara wasn't listening to me but to something inside herself.

"If you knew how much I admired her and then there we were fighting . . . I don't know why I took up with her in the first place.

"You know Erica is really a very honest person. I know, she was rough on you. But she wasn't pretending, that was the way she felt. Barbara, on the other hand... What Barbara said and what Barbara did were two different things. She was always pretending. America's sweetheart: What a pretense! Barbara was really a very nasty person.

"You know how I met her?"

"You told me a little bit this morning."

"When I joined JoAnne's club team, Barbara still didn't know who I was. I mean she didn't even remember me from High School. I was just somebody new, trying out. I didn't expect to play regularly, I was just trying desperately to be accepted as part of the team. And then, all of a sudden, I was a starter. And do you know why? Because Barbara thought I looked beautiful. Jolene, the girl I replaced, may not have been beautiful outside, but she was beautiful within. Jolene was a wonderful person. She helped me more than Barbara ever did. She practiced with me, helped me to be a better player, helped me to make the first team, and I took her place. Why?

"Barbara didn't care. Barbara didn't see things she didn't want to see. Jolene was part Mexican and as far as Barbara was concerned, Jolene didn't even exist.

"You know, I worshipped Barbara. I'd admired her all through high school. I'd worshipped her in college. Me the freshmen, she the senior. She was awful then, too. Why couldn't I have known that?

"You've heard the story about the tennis shoes. It's part of the legend. Barbara had picked out all the uniforms, color coordinated and then when the running shoes came . . .

"They were the wrong color."

"They were yellow on white when they should have been white on yellow. Something like that.

"So we had to have new shoes. But the company wouldn't take them back so we had to buy new shoes. Each of us, at $75 a pair. My parents had money, of course. What was $75? I didn't even think about the other kids. I just thought about myself in those days. You know how it was. But now that I'm older, I wonder what about the girls whose parents didn't have money. How could they afford it?"

"Barbara's parents had money, then."

"No, no, that's the funny part. They're dirt poor. I mean you wouldn't even want to live where Barbara lived or anything. I mean not that I'm a snob or anything. Not now. God, it must have been awful for Barbara in high school. It was awful for all of us."

"Not for you."

"Because, I'm pretty. I didn't know that in high school. Nobody does. Well, maybe Barbara did. Maybe we all do by the time we're seniors. But I didn't know that then. I think the only reason that Barbara was so self-confident in high school was that even then she'd kidded herself into believing she was a completely different person. I mean inside her head, she really thought she was somebody else complete with wealthy parents and a large house and terrible manners.

"Maybe, I was like that at first. But by the time I graduated, I was different. I cared about other people. Barbara, Barbara never changed, she was always the snob who put more emphasis on clothes than on the people who went inside them. And that's because I think deep down inside, Barbara hated Barbara so much that she'd already killed her and replaced her with somebody else. You know what I mean?"

I remembered the girl in the photograph, the eyes filled with suffering. I nodded.

“Why did I ever have anything to do with her?” Tears came into Sara eyes. With her eyes and nose slightly reddened with crying, Sara didn’t look as attractive as she usually did. Not much. I stayed with her while it got dark. I took her hand. She let me hold it. She wanted me to hold it. And after she left me with a swish of hips, I sat on the lawn with the young men, clutching to a dream.

Chapter 13

I'm basically an outdoors person. I used to live in Michigan and even on days when the groundhog couldn't find her shadow, I'd be outside soaking up the rays. Of course, there can be good reasons for not going outside. Like high winds and a chill driving rain. Like bruises up and down your body, a muscle spasm in your hip so you don't want to sit up, a big bruise on your tailbone so you don't want to lie back down again. So I stayed inside, disgusted with myself, telling myself over and over that I hadn't a clue, didn't know where to begin , wasn't getting the job done, etc., etc. Good reasons for staying home. And one more. Sara had rung early, asked how I was, and said she might be dropping by.

Marlene, that very special person, rang up also and asked how things were going. I told her, everything; I kind of dumped on her, in fact.

"Haven't a clue?" she questioned, "You seem to have lots of clues. It's just a question of picking out the murderer. Now let's start from the top."

I like my special person. She's a no-nonsense kind of woman. "JoAnne Greene," I said, "She had the opportunity and she had the motive."

"I don't see the opportunity. Sure her girls might cover up for her, at first. But don't forget, they were with her at the volleyball match watching her. She didn't have the opportunity to do anything unseen. And the same for her players, Potzie, Deborah. Sure a couple of them might have done anything JoAnne wanted them to do, even murder , with no questions asked and no regrets,. But not all of them. And the ones that weren't involved would be the first to rat on the others."

"I could check their stories," I began reluctantly. I guess I didn't want to go back to JoAnne Greene's house again.

"You should, now what's the motive?"

"Half a dozen of them. Good ones. Barbara had the power, JoAnne didn't. JoAnne used to be the big Kahuna, now Barbara was the star. And there's the problem of age. JoAnne probably used to be a lot prettier and a lot slimmer. Barbara was a symbol of everything JoAnne used to be."

My special person wasn't at all hesitant about contradicting me. "JoAnne is a media personality. People know her and remember her even when they don't know who the players are. She may not play anymore. But she can make or break players with her comments."

I was even less hesitant about contradicting. "JoAnne is a has been. Remember all that bull about her retiring from beach ball last year so she could devote more time to her coaching job. She didn't want to retire. She had to retire. She had no choice, her first place winnings had become eighth place and then no place at all. Sure, it could happen to anyone, but JoAnne's TV contract meant that she couldn't just walk away. She had to be there weekend after weekend watching younger women grab the glory. Every game she reported made it just that much more obvious how big the gap was between what she was and what she used to be."

"But why would she focus on Barbara? Barbara was a good player, but she's not the only good player."

"Just the number one beach player in the country. But I've got a better reason than that. Yesterday, Sara told me about JoAnne's semipro team, the one both Sara and Barbara had played for. Apparently, Barbara and JoAnne were constantly fighting for control."

"Sara? You saw Sara yesterday?"

"Yeah. Marvin the agent gave me this list of five suspects."

"I thought you'd already interviewed Sara at Erica's place. They live together you know."

"Erica is another strong candidate."

"Uh, huh. Look, I've got to back to work. You go interview your suspects or whatever it is you call them. A little rain won't hurt you."

"And the bruises," I said.

"Try Ben-Gay."

"You don't need to worry about Sara," I said by way of apology when I called Marlene back a half hour later. I'd gone out in the rain—she was right, it didn't hurt—and run the three short blocks to my office. I'd got soaked, of course, but there was a change of shirts in the clothes pile. My jeans, I just hung up over a chair to dry.

"I'm not worried," she snapped.

"I mean Sara has Erica."

"This week."

"I think it's pretty permanent."

"Uh, huh."

"Keep her guessing," Sara said from behind me. I jumped. How had she got into my office? "Hold on," I said into the phone. I put my hand over the receiver. "How did you get into my office?" I whispered to Sara.

"The door was open," she whispered back.

"What about the ..." I bellowed before I remembered I was supposed to be whispering. "I've got to go," I whispered into the phone.

"What?"

"I've got to go. Something has come up." I whispered hoarsely, keeping a wary eye on Sara's movements. After all, I was nude from the waist down.

"I can't hear you. Why are you whispering?"

I got it straightened out at last. Sara sat down quietly in the same chair I'd hung my pants on while I told Marlene about the two interviews I'd lined up for later in the day. Marlene said good, I wasn't giving up. I made kissing sounds into the phone and put the receiver down embarrassed.

Sara gave me a strange look. "You O.K." she said.

"Yeah. Yeah. Got a lot on my mind."

"You look nervous. Was that Marlene on the phone?"

"Yeah. No, stay there!" I hollered as Sara got up from her chair and strolled over to my desk. I slumped as far under the desk as I could and still see over the top.

"I was just going to straighten your collar," she said. "And have you got a pick or a hairbrush or something?"

"In my desk," I said. "I'll do it," I hollered when she started to reach over me.

"You're awfully nervous," she said leaning back against my wet pants, "Are you expecting Marlene to come over?"

"No, no," I said, "she's at work."

Sara rubbed her back against the chair moving her body erotically as she did so. A frown crossed her face and she stopped moving. "What are these?" She reached behind her and held up the wet pants. "You're not wearing any pants are you?" She grinned.

I nodded sheepishly. "The pantless detective." she continued, "Undercover work in nudist colonies our specialty. I wonder if you can help me?"

"It depends on the problem," I said and she burst into laughter.

"Do you have any dry clothes?"

"Just a pair of swimming trunks."

"Put them on. You look like a kid at her father's desk slumped down that way. Or a lowrider.

"Great legs," she continued, when I'd slipped on the trunks. "Seriously, I do have this problem."

"You're not here to see my legs, then?"

"No. I like you Phyllis, honest, but this is not why I came here. I'm worried about Erica."

"Ah this is a professional call. Well, let me just take a few notes." I got out a sharp pencil and a pad of paper and tried to look attentive. I didn't fool her or me for an instant.

"Oh, I do like you Phyllis. But Erica is my ... uh"

.".. special person," I finished for her.

"Uh, huh. You will help me won't you?"

"I'm on a case. I'll help you just as soon as it's wrapped up. Unless. Unless, the two are connected."

"I'm afraid. I'm afraid that it might have something to do with Barbara's killing."

She paused as if waiting to hear what I would say. I didn't say anything.

"Ever since, ever since Barbara died, Erica's been making strange phone calls. I mean she's never hidden anything from me and now she does, the phone calls, and she goes places in the morning."

"She goes to work," I said.

"No, she goes in earlier than she should. I called her at work yesterday, today too; she wasn't at work when she was supposed to be. She wasn't at home either."

"And you told her of your suspicions."

"She told me it was none of my business. We. . . we've always had an open relationship."

"And what do you want me to do?"

"I want you to follow her. I'll pay." She got out her purse.

"Give me a hundred dollars," I said. Did Sara think I was going to tell her to forget the money, no charge for a friend?

She gave me the hundred and kissed me, full on the lips. If it wasn't as good as the last time, it was because I wouldn't let it be. Sara Newcombe was a lot prettier than Derek Chzynski. But she was also an awful lot smarter. He'd started accusing other people the minute I'd backed him into a corner. Sara had snuck up on me, slowly, gradually. Confiding in me, pretending to confide in me, leaning her head on my shoulder that one time after she kissed me. She'd been planting clues. She could have been planting clues. Yesterday, she'd told me the story about JoAnne and Barbara quarrelling. Today, her story was about Erica's strange behavior. And it was all said so convincingly, so honestly, that I wanted to believe her. Had believed her. Would believe her again if her stories checked out.

A one-woman woman?

Chapter 14

I was out of suspects. At least I'd now gone once through the list that Marvin the agent had given me and come up a blank. Of JoAnne Greene, the affable if backbiting media personality, I knew just about as little as I did about anyone I'd seen on the tube. Actually, I'd learned more about JoAnne at the public library reading back issues of Volleyball Monthly than I had in our face-to-face interview. I knew that tough-as-nails Erica Mueller hated Barbara. But I also knew that in a head-to-head knockdown competition with Barbara over beautiful Sara Newcombe, it was Erica who'd won. I'd learned that Diane Purdy, suburban housefrau and tease, was not afraid to express her opinions. She was a straight shooter and (so her husband said) a crack shot. She also hated Barbara. Would she have poisoned her?

Derek Chzynski was a nice ordinary guy whose life had been totally stood on end by Barbara's murder. Maybe. Poison wasn't only a woman's weapon, it could also be that of a man who feels helpless inside. I thought he'd overplayed the role of the distraught fiancée. The women I'd interviewed said he was a mama's boy and maybe gay. Sara said he'd never taken a second look at her and that was proof enough he was gay in my book. Had Barbara been planning to leave him? A second meeting with Derek was called for. In fact, a second meeting with just about all of the suspects wouldn't hurt.

Maybe I should tail a couple of them as well. After all, one of them was clearly tailing me. But first I would have to persuade Marvin that a second round of interviews would produce the results he needed so quickly. Somehow, I didn't think he'd be so quick or so generous with his checkbook the second time around. If there was a second time.

It wouldn't make any difference. I was going to find Barbara's murderer whether or not I was paid. Barbara Dahl was, had been a wonderful person. There would never be another day on the beach, a day of sea and sand and sun when I would not think of her.

"You've interviewed her family, haven't you?" I thought back to the trusting look on Derek Chzynski's face when he'd asked me that question. Poor dumb Derek. Poor dumb me. No, Barbara, I hadn't called on your family before. But I was going to call on them now. Then, one by one, I was going to call a second time on each of the suspects and Marvin as well until I found your murderer.

If it had been anyone but "Barbie Doll" Dahl whose family I was visiting, I'd have known just from the address the kind of family she'd grown up in. 4012 Chapman Ave in Anaheim was biker country, home away from home to a street full of rednecks. While the rest of LA might be home to the fruits and the nuts, this was where the salt of the Southern earth came west to live and settle their prejudices with them.

Barbara's block had never known better days. It was jerrybuilt housing when it was thrown together in the forties and it was a lower-class white slum by the time 2002 rolled around. Mind you, Barbara Dahl's ancestral home was the best cared for house on the block. She hadn't forgotten her family when it came time to split up her winnings.

The aluminum siding was new. The slatted thermopane windows were new. The big, ten-foot high American flag over the front door was new. The house next door had made a valiant effort to keep up—it had a new paint job and a red tile walk, but clearly it didn't have the tournament money behind it that the Dahl's home did.

Close up, it looked as if the Dahl's home might have a new blacktop driveway too. It was hard to tell with the all the junk cars and motorcycles parked in front of the garage. I stepped up on the porch, a three-foot square slab of concrete with one white iron rail, and rapped on the front door. It opened slowly as in one of those horror movies, revealing a musty dark interior bare of furniture. And just as in the movies, no one was inside to greet me.

"Mrs. Dahl, Mrs. Dahl?" The sign on the doormat with the second American flag said, "walk right in neighbor," but I was reluctant. Maybe it was the two small signs in the porch window. The one read, "American Legion, I am a veteran and proud of it," the other "KKK," against a third small American flag.

"Mrs. Dahl?" Lengthen her legs, smooth out the wrinkles from her face, and take her back in time twenty or thirty years, and the apparition in front of me might have been Barbara Dahl, herself. As it was, my next best guess was that this was Barbara's mother.

"I'm sorry about your daughter's death, Mrs. Dahl."

"We all are," she replied. "Those damn niggers. They're killing everything, destroying everything."

I looked about me nervously. "If it's all right I'd like to come in and ask you a few questions."

"Barbara was a wonderful girl. She was an American. Would you like to see what she done for me?"

"Yes ma'am," I replied docilely. I followed Mrs. Dahl down the hall; an odor of must and decay was mixed with the more dominant scent of gasoline and roach killer. The room at the end of the hall had to be Mrs. Dahl's parlor. I recognized it from the memories of my own youth. A collection of glass dogs, throwaway pillows on the sofa, with "Souvenir of Louisiana" and "Orange County Fair" inscribed on them, and a tall glassed-in case filled with shelf after shelf of volleyball trophies, Barbara's trophies.

The wall was covered with photographs of Barbara—some professionally taken with her posing on the sand or against the wall of a studio. She could have been a model, I thought again. There were framed newspaper clippings, too, stained and faded. "Cerritos wins," "UCLA in Final Four," "Dahl is scoring leader." There were shots of Barbara accepting awards and team pictures, a dozen or more. Was that Sara?

"Barbara gave me this home," the woman said from behind me, sitting herself down heavily on the sofa. Her dress was clean and almost new, but the woman herself looked old and faded. If the mother was this ancient, how old must Barbara herself have been?

"She was my baby, the last and the best," the woman said as if reading my thoughts.

"Least you treated her like one." This last comment came from a muscular figure of Schwartzeneggian proportions who leaned insolently against the parlor wall, a gleaming metal wrench in his grease-stained hand. Like Derek Chzynski, this one too had muscles on his muscles, but there the resemblance to Derek ended. Pig eyes and a beer belly ruined the body builder effect. I was surprised I hadn't smelled his presence. On the whole, I'd rather have been alone with Derek in a dark alley. He'd have fought cleaner.

"Shut up George." Mrs. Dahl said.

"That's my baby, too," she said, turning to me with pride.

"Yes, ma'am."

"I had seven of them altogether. Lost three of them in the war."

"And two of'm in the penitentiary," snickered George.

"Shut up George. You came to see Barbara's trophies?" Mrs. Dahl said to me.

"Yes ma'am. I'm a private detective investigating her death."

"Well, there's no mystery about that. Haven't they arrested her yet."

"Who ma'am?"

"The nigger," George put in, "the wop nigger."

"We told her don't get involved with colored. But what can you do, they're everywhere these days."

"Yes, ma'am."

"Hey," the brute shouted, "you just going to stand around all day saying, 'yes ma'am' or what?"

I ignored him. "Ma'am, I've got a list of six suspects, I'd like to ask you about."

George yanked the notebook out of my hands. "Hey!" I said. I know V. I. Warshawsky would have punched George in the stomach, beat him with his own wrench and then stomped him to death. But "Hey!" was all I said. Sue me, I'm a coward with anyone larger than a small mountain.

"What are these chicken scratchings?"

"George, give the woman back her notebook."

"If you'll just give me a moment," I began, "I'll show you..." Too late, George was already ripping out pages as if they were daisy petals.

"Hah!" he hollered, "This is the one. deCastro. Says it all. She's a nigger, she's a wop, and she's a *de* Castro."

"I said to Barbara, 'honey, you got to stand up against them niggers,'" went on Mrs. Dahl oblivious to my pain.

"Wait a minute," I interjected, "Chara's a Guatemalan refugee."

"Chara?!" the ape said, "You her sweetie or somethin? And what's a Guatemalan if he ain't a nigger wop. What about them Contras?"

"It's all part of a conspiracy you see. Minute a real American girl rises to the top, why then they drag her down."

"Mama, she was getting mighty thin toward the end, partnering with a wop."

"But George, don't you see, they made her do it."

George had no answer to this paranoiac insight, so he turned on me instead, "You through asking questions, doll?"

"Well, I really need to ask your mother about..." I started to say.

"I say you're through," snapped George. "Take your notebook and go." He hurled the notebook at me and I caught it on the fly. It stung. They say a paper cut is the unkindest cut of all.

"Wait," I said as George put a big friendly paw on my neck and started to escort me out of the room. "I really need to ask Mrs. Dahl about Barbara's charities." I had turned to face Mrs. Dahl, but the pressure on my neck left me addressing the ceiling.

"She was a wonderful girl," Mrs. Dahl said, more to herself than to me, "All those things she done."

She had one of Barbara's testimonial plaques in her hand and was crooning over it the way a young child might embrace a small doll.

Pathetic? George soon brought me back to reality. "Barbara's Kids. Yeah, my sister was a regular do-gooder. But she was my sister, you know what I mean?" He shook me gently and my teeth rattled.

Hung up by the neck, he turned me slowly in the air, until my face was only inches from his beady eyes. "Now girl, if you don't arrest the nigger, why then I'm going to know who was laying down on the job. O.K.?"

"O.K." Did I say that? Was that me being agreeable? I thought I had more moral character.

"My sister was 100% American, maybe 98% toward the end. Those kikes and niggers did her in. And you're the one who's going to tell people who did it. O.K.?"

"O.K." This time it took more than lack of moral character to get out the words, it took the last of my remaining air. George's huge hand was tight and ugly on my neck. I wondered if he was leaving me with grease marks on my shirt or, at the least, with ring around the collar.

"Now. We got money. We're not poor. You got to believe Barbara left ma with plenty of insurance. You prove this de Castro did it. And I'll pay you double. Charo, hah!"

Sweet, elegant-even-when-bikini-clad Barbie Dahl related to this giant monkey? Darwin was wrong.

Chapter 15

From redneck country to ghetto, the investigation was beginning to take its toll in shirt collars and gas money. And the ghetto was where Dee-Dee Williams, the former Olympian and Barbara's one black friend lived. At least she was the only black friend of Barbara's that I knew about. Chara was in another class entirely.

I got off the freeway at one of those off-ramps where they warn white people never, never to run out of gas. I knew where I was going and I had a book of Thomas maps on the seat beside me, but you never know what can happen to your car.

Century Road went through and past the projects, through and past the bombed out remains of what must once have been a downtown. All the stores had heavy iron shutters. Young men lounged on the street corners jiving with one another and with the occasional woman who passed by. They may have had hard stares for me but, not knowing whether to play the innocent or the cop, I didn't look up.

Eventually, the projects gave way to streets that had never known the benefits of government reclamation, streets with trees and large, older homes. The lawns were freshly cut, some of the back yards had swimming pools, and in one block the houses had been replaced by rows of back-to-back two-story town houses and modern apartments, oops, sorry, condominiums. This was where the Buppies lived.

The kids playing in the street on bicycles and skateboards could have been typical suburban kids anywhere, except that their skin was black. Ditto for the fashionably dressed suburban matrons in jogging outfits and "Free to be you" hightops pushing their perambulators. I was out of place. They knew that, but were not about to reveal their feelings beyond a casual hostility.

The Williams' home wasn't the biggest on the block, but it was far from the smallest. It had a big front porch and a high front door. A basketball hoop waited for lay-ups over the garage and next to it one of those padded bars volleyball players use to practice spiking. I remembered the pint-size kid crawling on my Black Madonna's blanket. Dee-Dee had tall ambitions for her children.

A Mexican maid answered my knock. "You wait here," she said. The man who came to the door next in cardigan and slippers was a good six-feet five, six-feet seven. I could see why the Williams had selected a large older home. He couldn't have fit in one of those stucco shacks that are designed for midgets.

"Yes?"

"I'd like to talk with Dee-Dee Williams."

"Was she expecting you?"

"Not exactly," I said, "I just wanted to ask her a few questions."

"She's really awfully busy."

"It's part of an investigation. I'm working for the Professional Beach Volleyball Association."

"Dee-Dee doesn't play beach ball. Perhaps if the head of your Association were to phone her, we might arrange something."

"Charlie what's happening?" I heard another voice, a man's voice call from within.

"Excuse me one moment," the man said and stepped back in the house, I followed him two steps inside the front hallway and waited.

I heard him and the other man talking and laughing in the living room. As always when two black guys are talking and laughing close by, I wondered if they were talking and laughing about me.

Tall Charlie came back. "What are you doing inside my house?" he said.

"Why I ..." But there wasn't really much I could say to defend myself. Though I'd only taken a couple of steps inside, I wasn't sure why I was there myself. Would I have come in his house like that if he were white?

"Get out ... side please." He was trying hard to sound patient.

I got back on the porch.

"Have your boss call and make an appointment, all right?"

"Yes, Sir."

"Damn vagrants. The city has got to do something about all these homeless," I heard him call to his friend as he went back inside the house, closing the front door.

All the kids in the neighborhood seemed to be looking at me, watching me as I walked back to my car. The Buppie mothers stood defensively between me and their perambulators.

I wasn't going to steal anything. But I guess only I knew that.

I hoped the cops didn't pull me over. They get upset sometimes when they find a white gal in a beat up Plymouth driving through a well to do, all black neighborhood.

Chapter 16

You may have noticed that I'm not particularly successful in my face-to-face contacts. Interpersonal communications is just not my bag. The fact is that most of my detecting experience has been at staking out warehouses. On the whole I prefer it that way. You may not meet as nice a class of people. But there is less chance of being misunderstood.

Early the next morning, earlier than I think my tail was used to rising, I parked outside Erica Mueller's apartment building. It was a gray day when I arrived, a gray dawn, really, but by the time the first commuter had left the apartment building, the sun had come out and it promised to be another wonderful day in the Southland.

It was checking up time. Sure I believed Sara Newcombe or rather I wanted to believe her. But she wouldn't be the first person on a case that has lied to me.

Sara was the first of the two roommates to emerge from the building. She wore a green scarf over her hair, a long green coat that ought to have but didn't conceal her figure, and a well-worn pair of sandals. Still she was unmistakable as she hopped into a little orange Bug with VB-3 on its license plate and a Marina JC parking sticker in its back window.

Should I follow her? More than likely she was just off to school for a morning class. I decided to wait for her roommate. As far as I was concerned, Erica had always been the prime suspect.

With a roar of four furious sewing machines fighting for control, the Bug took off. Then silence. It was another half hour before Erica emerged. Again, there seemed to be the same halfhearted attempt at disguise, a muted Vera scarf over her hair, a formless gray coat, and a pair of low-heeled shoes. Again the silhouette—bosom like a ship's prow, broad hips, and long legs was unmistakable.

I could follow Erica, or I could try to break into her apartment. Deciding I could probably get away with both if my timing were right, I powered up my ancient Plymouth. Apart from a slight delay at the start—who would have believed that Erica would own a BMW—I had no trouble in tailing her, never really needing to stay more than a car length or two behind in the early morning commuting traffic. Still, I was completely unprepared when she stopped across the street from a nursery school, and pulled into the curb. I passed her car—there was no way I could stop in time—and also parked across the street from the school. I left several parked cars between the two of us, but stayed close enough that she could be glimpsed through my rear-view mirror.

For several moments, we both remained in our cars watching the kids playing in the schoolyard opposite. They all looked as if they were having fun; still, kids can go from laughter to tears in an instant. Two of the children particularly drew my attention, a short blond girl, three or four years of age, and a young boy, her brother judging by his features, who couldn't have been more than a year or two older. Despite the closeness in age, he acted more like her father or a doting uncle. They had been playing tag with the rest of the children when the girl's shoe came untied. The boy left the game to help his sister, not to tie her shoe—some words passed between them on this subject and apparently she wanted to tie it herself, but to offer advice and later his thumb as a platform for the final knot. They both seemed extremely pleased when the tying job was completed and the girl held out her tiny foot for his inspection.

I was pleased too. Pleased enough to want to shout to Erica two cars behind me how much I was pleased. But I restrained myself. We detectives try to be inconspicuous when we're under cover.

Someone came to the door of the school then, an adult, and called to the children. The boy looked up with a bright smile of anticipation, the girl looked sad. The boy said something to the girl that I could not hear. She looked disappointed. He carefully adjusted the buttons on the her jacket, acting for all the world as if he were fifty instead of five. Then he gave her a peck on the cheek and ran off toward the school.

I heard a gasp from nearby, and saw Erica in my rear-view mirror, half in and half out of the BMW; she was crying. She started across the street, calling "Johnny." It was too late, the boy had already started toward the school.

"Susie?" The little blond girl looked up at Erica. She smiled and started toward the fence. The boy ran back and caught her arm. The girl stopped. The two of them looked at Erica who looked back at them through the wire grating.

Then the adult who had come out on the steps called to them again, this time calling them by name, "Johnnie, Susie." The boy turned around and taking his sister's hand walked toward the school.

The girl followed reluctantly, looking back over her shoulder every few steps. "Mommy," she may have said; I couldn't tell, I was too far away.

After awhile Erica got back in her car and drove away. I stayed for a while watching the squirrels who had returned to the now empty school yard, but they were no fun. Then I drove away myself.

These were the wrong secrets I had learned. There had to be a better way.

Chapter 17

"Barbara's Kids, living testimony that volleyball is a sport that cares."

from materials provided by the Five Star Talent Agency.

Barbara's Kids may have been a shtick, thought up by a conniving press agent, but it also may have been the real Barbara, the poor kid out of her depth at a rich kid's school, trying to give others what she herself had missed. Anyway, I wanted to see for myself.

The description I'd been given was of a halfway house for older orphans that hadn't been (and wouldn't be) adopted and were too young still to go out on their own. I don't know what I was expecting exactly, leering juvenile delinquents brandishing their switchblades on the stairwells, but it wasn't the Donnie and Marie show. And Donnie and Marie was exactly what I got. Four kids in skirts or long pants and neatly starched blouses. That is, the girls—one with long blond hair, and one a brunette with a Marie Osmond haircut, wore blouses. The two boys, so similar they might have been twins, wore ties and shirts with stiff collars and looked for all the world like Mormon ambassadors coming up your walk. Except that they sat stiff and quiet in chairs like part of a photograph from Architecture Digest, the boys with books in their hands, the girl with the long hair working on some embroidery.

One boy smiled at me when I walked into the room; the other, about fifteen, seemed devoted to his book or rather to a small model car that he ran back and forth over the book's surface. He stopped only when the first boy took him by the arm and pointed to me, and then he simply stuck the car under the book and continued to turn pages without looking up.

The girl with the embroidery was doing her best to outline a printed flower with needle and thread, but her needle kept missing so that the thread went up and over and sometimes across the design itself. I smiled. Too shy to look up, she continued working. They were all shy, shyer than normal kids should have been and far quieter, I thought.

They were Barbara's Kids, good-liking, quiet, and dull. The sort of kids you'd think would be almost anyone's first choice for adoption. But the dullness was in their eyes too and I realized at once why the blond had so much trouble with her embroidery, the pudgy one played with his car, and the girl with the pixie haircut picked at the words in the book she'd clearly read oh so many times before.

As if to show how wrong and how right first impressions can be, the alert boy got out of his chair and walked across the room to where I was standing. He took my hand and shook it, a firm manly handshake. "Hi, I'm Brett," he said in a newly acquired deep voice. But before I could reply, he'd scuttled back to his chair, face flaming, and was soon as quiet as the other three.

From farther inside the house, I heard the sound of children, real children yelling and a female adult making threatening sounds in reply. As the noise increased, the four figures in the front room began to fidget in their chairs, though remaining silent themselves. Finally my active friend with the smile couldn't stand it any longer. He got up from his chair and walked to where I was standing, "Hi, I'm Brett," he said a second time in his deep voice and shook my hand again.

“I like you Brett,” I said quickly, before he could scuttle away. All four children looked up at me then and the girl with the pixie haircut even made eye contact. “Hi,” I said to her. “Hi,” she replied, shyly.

Before we could begin to talk, two turbulent figures burst into the room. A boy about fourteen, with an excess of black hair tumbling forward over his forehead, and a girl a year or two younger. Though the boy wore the stiff white shirt that seemed to be the uniform in that institution, I was pleased to see he had a black smudge on his collar and a crayon mark under the pocket. He might have imagined himself James Dean, but a slight cast to one eye left him looking more like Robin Williams as Popeye. His girl friend—an unrequited love one could see at a glance—was still undeveloped, but beginning to shoot up if not out—Olive Oyl for sure.

The two were fighting over a small black bear with one ear that the boy was waving over his head. The girl was jumping up and down reaching for the bear and giggling each time she collided with the boy. As she was already an inch or two taller than he, I suspected she wasn’t trying very seriously. They were beautiful kids. All kids are or could be, I thought.

Meanwhile, the unequal struggle continued. I’m sure Olive would have regained the bear eventually without violence, had a gray-haired woman not then burst into the room and begun to tussle with the boy. The woman’s face was a study in meanness; I was not surprised to see actual blows exchanged. But her mean look changed to an ingratiating smirk when she saw me standing by the door.

“Oh,” the woman said in a fruity voice, “we have company.” The boy looked up, his face running quickly through an entire gamut of emotions, hope, bravado, embarrassment, antagonism—and, just for an instant, bravado, and hope again. Conscious of his shortness, he moved back a step, so he could get a good look at me. The bear forgotten, fell to the floor.

"Are you from the estate?" the woman asked.

"I'm doing an investigation," I replied evasively.

"I'm sure you'll find that everything is in order. We're doing an essential job here. All the children are as grateful as they can be. Aren't you children?"

The four children in the armchairs stood up as they'd obviously been taught to. There was a weak chorus of "yeses," though only the voices of Popeye and Olive could be heard clearly. "We like it here," Popeye said.

My friend Brett got up from his armchair and walked over to me.

"Hi. I'm Brett," he said.

"I like you Brett," I said quickly, before he could leave.

"Brett's O.K.," Popeye said reassuringly, if unnecessarily in my case. He took Brett's arm with a surprising gentleness and helped him walk back to the other room and out of the way.

"You're not going to close the home are you?" said the woman.

Mentally, I slapped myself. Why had I lied or rather why had I not told the truth about myself when asked if I was with the estate?

I should have been up front and told her then that I was investigating Barbara's murder. These people had too much at stake here. I wanted to say, "If it was up to me lady, these kids could stay here forever." But what if they did close the home and who was to say they would not? Whatever I said now would be wrong. Before I could even begin to stammer an apology, Popeye cut the ground out from under me, completely.

"You're just doing your job, right lady?" He smiled, so help me as if he and I were golfing buddies.

"Look. If it was up to me, you kids could stay here forever. I don't know. I just don't know. It probably depends on Barbara's will. You should ask the lawyer."

My voice was gruff, gruffer than it should have been. Without Barbara's spark behind beach volleyball, they probably would close the home or have to search awfully hard for another sponsor. I couldn't tell these kids that.

The quiet boy who'd been playing with the toy automobile began to cry. The others gathered around him, Brett, Olive, Popeye. Why was the kid crying? The only one in the room who could pass for Bluto was me and I would be leaving soon.

A third figure, a short, out of breath, fat boy burst into the room. It had to be Wimpy. "Where's my bear?" he said.

"Here it is Todd," said Olive retrieving it from the floor and handing it to him.

"You shouldn't have stolen my bear," he said to Popeye reproachfully.

"I apologize Todd," Popeye said, clearly watching for my reaction to this manly gesture.

"I'm sorry, I ripped up your picture," Wimpy-Todd said.

"What!" Popeye lost all control. In a way, I liked him better that way, but I had to reach out my big hand and grab his wrist to stop him from hurting the smaller boy. The kids all looked at me again with that sad expression on their faces. Me, Big Bad Bluto. I rubbed my face as if somehow I'd acquired whiskers.

"It's all right," the woman said to me, "You can let him go. Greg has this photograph of Ms. Dahl he keeps under his mattress. We can get him another one. Todd, you know Greg loved that picture.

"I loved my bear," Todd said. "Besides, Ms. Dahl was no good. You know she didn't like us. You know that. She only liked the dummies."

"Todd!"

Again I had to restrain Greg. The room was pandemonium all over again; this time, three of the kids were crying.

"I'm sorry," the woman said, "It's really time for their lunch. They like to help me fix lunch, particularly the girls." At a signal, the four from the front room got up and followed the woman into the back, the girl with the pixie haircut still clutching her book.

This left only the three of us in the front room. "You take that back Todd," Popeye said.

"It was true."

"You take that back," he said again menacingly.

"Let's play dominos," Olive said, I thought quite sensibly.

"She liked all of us," Popeye said almost pleadingly, "We were her special kids."

"Baloney. She wasn't my mother," said Wimpy. "Besides she was gay. She only liked weird stuff. Do you like opera? Do you want to go to a bunch of museums?"

"She took us to the movies."

"Yeah, how often? She didn't take me. She took Marilyn. She took Renee. She just wanted to be with the dummies."

"Renee's not a dummy. She's just slow."

"Who's Renee?" I took the opportunity to ask Olive. I noticed she hadn't allowed herself to be drawn into the argument, and was curious which side she was on.

"She's the one with the beautiful long hair," Olive said.

"It's long, all right," I said, "but I'm not sure it's as pretty as yours."

She blushed.

"What are you two talking about?" Popeye interrupted.

"Things," Olive replied.

"What kind of things?"

"Just things."

“Tell me,” I began, for I saw that at last that I had their complete attention, “Did you three ever hear anything about Ms. Dahl wanting to adopt a couple of you kids?”

Instead of replying, Popeye, that is Greg, threw open the front door and stepped out on the porch. I followed him, the other two close behind.

Greg fidgeted from one foot to the other, but he didn’t move. He obviously had something he wanted to say to me but was having difficulty getting it out. The other two stepped back, showing a degree of insight that I’d have thought far beyond their age.

“She was wonderful. She did everything she could for us kids. It doesn’t matter if we can’t stay here anymore. Nothing matters.” With an abrupt movement, he swung out over the railing and was off down the street.

“Greg,” the girl called after him. But Greg didn’t even look around. “He needs love.” she said.

“Hey,” I said, “Is he supposed to do that? Shouldn’t we tell someone he’s taken off?”

“He’ll be back,” the fat kid said, “He always comes back. He was in love with her you know.”

“He was not.” said the girl.

“Was too.”

“Was not!” She burst into tears.

The fat kid knew he’d gone too far, but he didn’t know what to do about it. I’d been there a couple of times myself. The fat kid looked at me. “Was too,” he said, and ran back into the house.

This left me and the crying girl standing on the front steps, with me looming over her like some kind of monster. I sat down on the step beside her. It seemed the right thing to do. After awhile, she sat down, too.

The surrounding neighborhood was beautiful or had been once, lined with single-family houses, like Barbara’s own, only better kept. That most of the faces in the area now had slanted eyes or dark skins was the only way you could tell the neighborhood had changed. Somehow the area hung together; we, the children and I, were the only ones that were now out of place.

Olive looked at me now, still without words, the way it had been the other day when I was sitting on the lawn with Sara. Maybe, some day this girl would be like Sara, too. Maybe not. It would take a lot of changes.

Unlike Sara, when she talked finally, she talked to me, not through me, and not by playing back some prerecord tape she played for everyone.

"She didn't like Greg. Ms. Dahl didn't. And he liked her a lot. Used to talk about how he was going to marry her when he grew up. Crazy talk. But she didn't like him. She used to take him along with us because I liked him.

"She used to take us all to the movies. I like the movies. It's better than on TV even if it's the same thing. You know what I mean?

"But she wouldn't sit next to him. Greg wanted to, every time. Maybe once he sat next to her. I switched with him. He asked me to. But she made me switch right back."

"She sat next to you in the movies?"

"Me or Dora. She liked us the best." The girl looked up at me defiantly.

There was a lot more I wanted to ask her, but what the hell, what did it matter now? I thanked the kid, offered her a dollar that she refused, offered her ten dollars so that both Greg and she could go to the movies, which she took, and walked to my car.

"She needed love," I thought I heard her call after me. "We all do," I mumbled under my breath.

I should have been paying attention to the street.

A half dozen cars had been parked at the curb when I first pulled up. Now, only one remained, a long, stretched out limousine, the kind pimps use. I heard the limo's engine start, but it still came as a surprise when I stood face to face with the car—its black chauffer looking horrified behind the wheel. I dived for the curb, didn't make it; the limo's fender grazed my hip. When I looked up, the limousine was still moving, its black-capped driver not even bothering to look back. The limo was followed a moment later by a silver-gray motorcycle, its rider in crash helmet, leather jacket and bikini bottoms revealing an incredible expanse of gleaming brown leg as the cycle whipped on by.

"Are you all right?" Olive asked.

Even my follower had followers.

Chapter 18

I've always been grateful for the late shift at the foundry. A mobile canteen is usually parked outside even after the restaurants in my area are closed. I got a burrito and a cup of coffee from it. The burrito was left over from the day shift, I think, but at least it was warm. So was the coffee.

I didn't have time to tend to my bruises; it wouldn't have done any good anyway. The photograph of Barbara sat on my desk watching me accusingly. I'd bought a two-dollar frame for it, the kind they sell at K-Mart that comes with a picture of mountain scenery already under the glass. When are you going to find my killer, Phyll?

The telephone rang. It was Mike. Mike? Mike Purdy, Diane's husband. I hadn't really expected to hear from him again, but apparently he'd had a long suppressed fantasy of being a detective. I had a long suppressed fantasy about a little home in the suburbs and a loving redhead at the door waiting to greet me each day when I got home. Maybe we should switch. But I didn't say what I thought out loud.

"I've got a list of names for you," he said.

Just what I needed, more suspects. "Thanks," I said flatly.

He read them out the names to me: "Peggy James," "Keesha Doksum,," ... I didn't recognize any of them.

"Who are they?" I asked.

"These are girls that were bumped from teams after Barbara came aboard."

I wasn't pleased. "Then your list doesn't include girls who merely thought Barbara had bumped them or kept them from joining clubs or stolen their boyfriends. Mike, this is garbage. Were any of these people at the finals on the beach?"

My sarcasm was wasted. "I'm not sure," he said, "but we could check. I'm running a check on the demographics, now.""Demographics?" God, I hate amateurs. And Mike really was a nice guy.

"Age, race, socioeconomic status, gay or bi, single or married, that sort of thing."

Demographics. "Are any of them nuts?" I asked.

"Nuts?"

"Nut cases, star persons. Are they crazy? Have they been in mental institutions or do their neighbors think they ought to be locked up? Face it, anybody who gets upset enough to kill somebody over what happened in junior high has got to be pretty weird."

"No, the list I gave you is just the people she bumped off club teams."

"Check it out," I said wearily.

"Sure."

That ought to keep him busy. Demographics! What did Mike think I was doing, running a campaign for City Council?

Of course, I was really only mad at myself. Three and a half days of investigation and what did I have to show for it? One bizarre but insanely pleasurable sexual encounter, and three close misses (fantasy wise). A new male friend Mike (possibly). A new female friend Sara (possibly). A visit with some really wonderful kids, and three sets of bruises at the hands of so-called adults. Maybe a case of the crabs, I don't know. Oh yes, and six fewer suspects than I'd had at the beginning.

What did I know, that I didn't know before? Notebook please.

Witness and suspect number one: JoAnne Greene, media personality and former beach volleyball champion. Had a kind phrase for everyone with just a small dose of arsenic in the middle. Arsenic? Was my subconscious trying to tell me something?

Witness number two, Erica Mueller, a big woman with a strong resemblance to my ex. God, how I would like to pin the murder on her (or my ex for that matter). But she wouldn't poison someone. She'd cut them up in little pieces and drain their blood first. Unless, ... they were a little boy and girl whom she loved.

Diane Purdy, the all-American girl. Nah. She was too clean cut. (Mike her husband wasn't clean cut, but I'll bet dollars to his doughnuts, that he hadn't put the poison in the water bottle. He would have to have left his chair at the computer terminal, and he obviously never did that even to make love. Men have all the luck.) Still, Diane for all her relaxed easy-going attitude, could get upset fast. Especially when Barbara's name came up.

Witness and suspect number four, Chara, the nature girl, from Guatemala or Cuba, or wherever. Nah, nah, no.She was just too nice. What had I learned from talking to her? That words aren't really necessary. I wondered if she drove a motorcycle.

Witness and suspect number five, Sara Newcombe, the knife artist. Sara said she was innocent, and I believed her. Besides, the killing should have gone the other way round, with Barbara killing Sara because Sara had dumped her. And I'm willing to bet that Barbara, like Derek, would have broken down and cried before killing anything that beautiful.

Witness and suspect number six, Derek Chzynski. Momma's boy or stud depending on who (or whom) you asked. He said he loved Barbara and I kind of believed him. And I just couldn't see him using poison when a headlock from his powerful muscles would have done the job so much quicker.

Ditto for witness and suspect number seven, Bo-Bo the apeman, Barbara's brother. A head smash with an axe handle was more his style. And he would kill on impulse not planning.

Barbara's mother? Nah, child poisoning went out with Medea.

That left...Barbara's Kids. They loved her and hated her, like most people. But they didn't have wheels. And the killer obviously did. I had bruises to prove it.

Which left...no suspects whatever. Which put me even up with the police if you could believe the newspapers.

About this time, I started doing something you're not supposed to do during a murder investigation: I started wondering whether the murder victim had been a good person or a bad person. On the whole, I decided that Barbara Dahl had been a bad person. Not because of anything that had been said about her. To the contrary, none of the people I'd interviewed had said Barbara Dahl was a bad person, Wimpy's complaints about opera and art museums aside. It was just that no one had said she was a good person either.

JoAnne Greene, who'd had a good or bad word (mostly bad) about almost everyone in the game, had been almost totally silent on the subject of Barbara. Sure, JoAnne had talked a lot about how Barbara had won this tournament and placed second (to her, JoAnne) in the next one, but she hadn't said "Gee whiz, volleyball will never be the same now that Barbara is gone." No one had. Marvin the agent was the only one who'd said he'd miss Barbara and I knew he was merely referring to his fee.

Erica hadn't said a bad word about Barbara. In fact, those were Erica exact words, "I haven't got a bad word to say about her." So all of Erica's bitching at the tournament was just her way of letting off steam. Or was Erica's the sort of language that all Barbara's friends and opponents ended up using?

Even Derek, the loving boyfriend, the strong man in tears, had he loved Barbara or the image? I hadn't heard any long loving speeches about Barbara's endearing qualities, just a lot of anger about whoever had messed up Derek's own plans.

Diane Purdy has been somewhat negative. Well, a lot negative. "Stuck-up no-good bitch" were her exact words. And the incident of the tennis shoes from years and years ago, still bugged her. It seemed to have bugged a lot of people, Sara included. Maybe I should have asked Sara for more details. I should call on her again. Maybe Erica wouldn't be home this time? Naaa.

I did a first in my detecting career at this point. I called on my significant other, notebook in hand. She was surprised, and pleased. "You want to interview me!"

What I heard from Marlene about Barbara surprised me. Not just the content, but that all this time my very special person could have concealed such strong feelings from me.

Turned out that Barbara was your typical little girl in every sense of the word (even at 6' 1"): when she was good she was very, very good; when she was bad, she was horrid. Barbara was very good when she was on the court. Thousands of sports fans knew that, had known that. If you were her partner, or her coach, or a member of her team, she was good. She'd share the credit and she'd share the kills. (She'd had to be a team player, of course; volleyball has no room for super stars; too much happens too fast.)

On the court, Barbara was the perfect team player. On the court, Barbara was always your friend. But off the court? Watch your back. The key, and I'd learned this from my friend Mike the computer whiz, was that a talent like Barbara got to pick and choose who she'd have on her team. When Barbara spoke (or lisped as JoAnne put it), coaches listened.

Barbara had her prejudices, as the Purdy's had said. If you didn't wear the right clothes or do your hair in the "in" style, then you didn't play on Barbara's team. Marlene said Barbara had been making coach's picks for them as far back as high school.

Even at USC where there is absolutely no shortage of volleyball talent, Barbara had managed to make her presence felt, enough to keep one girl off the team, enough to make sure another girl, a Eurasian they'd lured from the Philippine national team, didn't have her scholarship renewed.

In short, Barbara Dahl, the golden-haired princess whose portrait still hung over my desk, was an unmitigated bitch and Klansman in disguise. Despite her superficial popularity, she was generally hated (and feared) by everyone, including, in the end, her own immediate family. What little Olive Oyl had said, "I tried to like her," went for even the best intentioned. But Barbara Dahl had a tongue so acid, she couldn't keep a partner in bed or on the court. Eventually and predictably, the only one who would play ball with Barbara was a nymphomaniac who couldn't understand a word of English.

Such was Barbara Dahl, America's pride and joy and the universal symbol of beach volleyball. Marvin, I fear you made a terrible mistake. But Marvin wasn't asking for my advice on his public relations campaign. He'd hired me to find a murder. So I'd find away.

But there were no more suspects, no more witnesses. I could look over the tapes the T.V. people had taken of the game. After all there were shots that hadn't appeared on T.V. as well as the shots that had. Or . . . , wait . . . , maybe there was a witness, one I'd forgotten about. Maybe, I'd got the numbering wrong. JoAnne Greene wasn't witness number one. I was. Like Marvin had said, I was the best witness they had. I'd been sitting only four feet away from where the murder was committed. I'd even read the label on the poisoned water bottle. Quick, quick what else had I seen?

Chapter 19

When the telephone rang, I could see the killer's face before me, could see each detail of the actual crime as I'd seen it that day on the beach. I reached for the telephone. It was Marvin.

"We're having a party," he said. "We want you to come."

"What?" I replied stupidly. For the past twenty-four hours, I'd been anticipating and dreading this phone call. Too much time had passed since Barbara Dahl was killed. Marvin would want an end to the investigation, now. And now I was sure I had the killer. Almost sure. If only I had another evening, another half day.

"I need another half day," I said into the receiver.

"Of course, of course," he replied, soothingly. "No problem. I knew you were going to need more time. But that's part of the reason for this party. Most of the people who knew Barbara will be there and all of the prime suspects. You'll be able to talk to them all in one place. Clever huh."

"Marvin, how am I going to talk to anyone at a party? What do I do, invite them one at a time into the library to confess? Nobody will want to talk to me. Besides, they'll all be half blasted. You're going to serve liquor aren't you?"

"Two bars," Marvin replied proudly, "a band, and a d.j. to play records in between. Come on. You'll have fun, you'll help raise money for Barbara's Kids—that's the real reason for this party, and you're sure to catch a killer."

This was not the way Miss Marple went about solving crimes. Although, the fund-raising party did mean I had more time to work on the case. "When?" I asked.

"About fifteen minutes from now. I tried to get you most of the day, but this is the first time I caught you in. You should get an answering service."

"I've got an answering machine," I snapped.

"But have you listened to it?"

Forty-five minutes later, that very special person in my life and I pulled up in front of Marvin's elegant split-level home. It was still a little before nine and who ever went to a party before nine in this town? Professional athletes and show people who had responsibilities the next day. The quarter-mile of driveway was already packed with Porsches and BMW's. Just as well that I had to park a block and a half away. My ancient Plymouth wouldn't have fit in.

Marvin's multilevel home was straight out of Fantasy Island, Olympic-size swimming pool, cabana and all. He didn't have a front door, he had a gateway out of some medieval castle. Glass cases near the entrance held a collection of rare seashells; hidden spotlights in the garden lit up a series of statues—each one a reproduction of a famous museum piece.

The place was alive with noise and music. There were speakers everywhere, including the bathrooms and you had to shout to make yourself heard. I couldn't believe the size of the dining hall. Just as Marvin had described on the telephone, it had been turned into a dance floor, with two bars at one end and a band at the other.

Everyone who was anyone in the world of volleyball was there: Mike Dodd, Sinjin Smith, and Tim Hovland from the men's pro beach circuit, Laura Kessel and Julie Maginot from the ill-fated women's professional volleyball league, and a host of other athletes and minor celebrities. You didn't have to be a volleyball buff to recognize Karch Kiraly and Steve Timmons. I wondered if they'd brought their Olympic gold medals with them.

I recognized a lot of people I'd never really expected to see again. Erica was dancing with Steve Timmons. As large as she was in real life, she looked small and cuddly in the big redhead's arms. I gave Erica a big smile; she scowled and turned away. I saw Sara, she smiled. I saw Derek and Diane Purdy. All that was missing from the scene were the kids—Popeye and Olive that I'd met this afternoon, and I wouldn't have been surprised to see them waiting on tables.

Barbara Dahl was missing of course. But then, this party was supposed to be a wake. A wake for a dead American princess. We shouted and made noise because we missed her so, and because we were so glad to be alive ourselves.

"Do you want to dance?" I asked that very special person in my life; other same-sex couples were already on the floor.

"What?" she replied absently, or maybe she just couldn't hear me. She seemed completely freaked out by it all.

"This place is one big speaker cabinet," I said, unable to keep still.

"Do you want to dance?" a warm feminine voice whispered in my ear.

"It's Sara," I shouted to Marlene, "Do you mind if I dance with her?

"She's a suspect," I added when that very special person didn't reply.

"Suit yourself," she said nonchalantly and let go of my hand.

I took Sara in my arms and we danced into the crowd.

"I'm glad you came," she said.

"You'd have plenty of partners," I said. I gestured with my head toward the end of the room by the band, where a dozen or more women danced with one another.

"I'm very selective. So is Erica. She likes you incidentally."

"Me!"

"She thought you liked her, too. In fact, we both were wondering if you were going to find some excuse to call her back."

"She threw me out of the house!"

"Oh, that was because she didn't want to talk about Barbara. Don't let that discourage you."

We danced without speaking. I wondered why I liked Sara so much. I mean if we weren't going to do anything or anything. I don't think she knew what I was thinking, because she picked up the conversation in kind of a strange place. "Some volleyball players are gay, some aren't. Most aren't. Or most are. I wouldn't know.

"There's Diane Purdy. She's married."

The freckled cherub went by only a few yards away. She waved.

"That's not her husband," I said, pointedly.

"Oh, he doesn't dance. He doesn't even go to parties. I'll bet she came here alone."

"Sounds promising."

"Forget it. You can dance with her if you like. But it won't do you any good. She's crazy about her husband.

"And there's another example. Dee-Dee Williams. She's even got a couple of kids."

"Dee-Dee Williams?"

"The black girl. To my left. She was in the Olympics."

"The Olympics! I've heard about her. Is she really the greatest female player in the world?"

All I could see was the back of Dee-Dee's head, but I thought I recognized the black guy she was dancing with. I'd noticed him earlier. Very smooth on his feet. He gave me a wink when he saw the way Sara was clinging to me. I saw the way Dee-Dee burrowed up against his shoulder and gave him a wink right back.

"I'd like to meet Dee-Dee. Is that her husband?" I asked.

"I don't think, so." Sara replied. "Her husband's a really good looking guy. The guy she's with is handsome, all right, but her husband's even handsomer. Can you believe it? Some of these black guys."

"Some of these black girls."

"Hah, you'll have more luck with me, than you'll have with Dee Dee. She's not crazy about white guys or white girls."

"Or white people," I added.

"Right."

The band switched to a twist. I knew how to twist. So did Sara. The black couples stayed but a lot of the other couples dropped out.

"You know Erica was married once." Sara said.

"A black guy?"

"No, silly. He's some kind of an accountant. They were married almost six years. She's even got two children."

"But she doesn't have custody."

"No. She's not very happy about that."

Sara didn't ask how I happened to know about the children and I didn't volunteer any more information. The twist came to an end but the music segued quickly into another noisier tune. "Another?" Sara asked.

"I should be back with Marlene," I said, nodding toward my table.

"Save me another dance then?"

"Sure!" It was nice to be popular.

As I walked back, I thought I saw Chara leaning against the wall watching the dancers. It was hard to be sure, all I could really see were long black legs in a long white dress slit up the side. When I looked a second time, she was gone.

"You want to dance?" I said to that special person.

"In a moment. There's something I want you to see, first. A lot's been happening while you were gone."

"Like what?" I asked.

“See the girl in the black dress? Don’t be so obvious. The one with all the sequins?”

When I looked where she’d been pointing, I saw a plain, almost dowdy girl in a sequin-studded black dress. She had thick legs, a Carol Burnette face, and a body that seemed terribly out of place in the group of young athletes around her. The dress did nothing for her appearance. And the little mirrors on the dress only made her look ridiculous.

“That’s Valerie. I used to work with her. Well, her husband is dancing with that girl over there.

“Don’t be so obvious,” she said again when I started to twirl around, though there was no way I could see behind me without turning. The girl she’d pointed to was a striking redhead, tall, and very full in the chest.

“I like that one,” I began and received a kick to my heel in reply.

“That’s Potzie’s sister, she’s down visiting from...”

“Potzie?” I interrupted. “I know a Potzie.”

Oh, God did I know. Potzie, the blond from JoAnne Greene’s living room, the female creep who’d suckered me into a game of volleyball, blindsided me, then kicked me as I lay on the gymnasium floor, was deep in conversation with Valerie, the Carol Burnette type. Potzie looked very mammalian in a too tight sleeveless black jersey, no sequins, but I wasn’t going to be taken in twice.

“What do you suppose she sees in him?” Marlene said.

“Who she? Who him?” I replied. There were too many characters in this little soap opera.

“Valerie’s husband!”

Oh, yes, the one dancing with the redhead. Who ever looked at men anyway? Balding, stoop-shouldered, and pudgy, he was no match for the redhead. He was barely good enough for his wife.

"Potzie's sister has been making a play for him all evening. I had plenty of time to watch them when you deserted me. See they're dancing together, now. While Valerie is talking with Potzie. I bet Valerie is asking her to get her sister back to San Jose as fast as possible.

"She's kind of a plain jane." I meant Valerie.

"And what about him?" Marlene would like it if men and women were judged by more equal standards.

"I still don't know who you mean. Do you want to dance?" I asked.

"Sure. I thought you'd never ask."

I thought I had but some people you just don't argue with.

Dancing with that very special person was every bit as good as dancing with Sara, maybe even a little bit better. After all we'd had more practice. Maybe Marlene and I ought to do this more often. Go to parties where there was dancing or find some club where couples like us danced instead of just sitting around listening to music.

"It's them," she said.

"Who?" I whispered. More soap opera?

"The guy behind us and the sister," she hissed back.

"I don't care," I said. Close up the guy looked worse than he had from a distance. The body was soft, and his loose lip and frenetic grin left the impression of a ventriloquist's dummy on wheels. The redhead was still outstanding.

The black guy and Dee-Dee came our way again. He gave me another wink.

When we got back to our table, Marvin was hovering like a maitre d'. "You kids looked great on the dance floor. I bet you've been dancing together a long time. Have you?"

I looked at Marlene; she looked at me; "Yes we have," we both said at once.

"And what are you doing now? Sitting this one out?"

"Don't ask," I said, "there's this soap opera."

We filled him in quickly on the details, with my special person adding some bits I'd missed the first time around.

"Oh, Valerie," Marvin said, "She works in the office. I think she's quitting. She says she found a better job."

I felt a hand on my shoulder and looked up to find Sara standing in back of me. Marlene gave her and me a look that meant, "once is fun, twice is pushing it." I tried to pretend I hadn't noticed Sara, but she continued to stand there, pulling on my arm till I had no choice but to stand up and let myself be dragged away.

"This is not a good idea." The last angry look I'd gotten from Marlene had made it clear I'd already spent too much time with Sara.

"Erica wants you to call her," Sara said breathlessly once we were out of earshot of the table.

"She does?"

"Will you call her?" I shrugged. "Good. And tell that special person of yours that I'm sorry I had to drag you away."

So was I. When I got back to our table, Marlene refused to make eye contact, even though it was obvious she was desperate for an escape from Marvin's latest monologue.

The three girls—Potzie, Valerie, and Potzie's sister, were now sitting together. The sister from San Jose was crying, heaving great sobs, and Valerie seemed to be trying to comfort her. The husband was nowhere to be seen. Probably breaking some other girl's heart.

But it was All My Children with a twist. I watched as Valerie and the predatory mammal ascended the stairway hand in hand. Potzie's sister dried her eyes as the husband came over to the table to console her. What a dork.

Meanwhile, Marvin's pointless anecdote ground to its predictable end. I think my special person was asleep. "We're going," I said. "Goodbye Marvin."

"Hey, the party is just getting started. I want you to circulate."

"I've circulated. Four times around the dance floor. And I'm not really getting to talk to anybody. That was the purpose in my coming here wasn't it? That and raising money for Barbara's Kids."

"It's the atmosphere," he said, waving his arms, "the atmosphere, you'll get to know these people better once you see them with their hair down."

"I've seen them with their hair down, sweat in their armpits, and sand in their trunks, so what? You told me this party was a tribute to Barbara, to raise money for Barbara's Kids. I haven't heard one mention of the Kids—they're wonderful, or of Barbara. I think that people have totally forgotten about her and that they never really cared in the first place."

"You may be right," Marvin began.

"I care." I interrupted. "I'm going to find her killer."

"Ease up," Marvin said, slapping my arm. "Life goes on. Let's talk, O.K. I should go over your notes anyway. Maybe tomorrow. Next week at the latest." He walked away.

"Marvin!" I called after his retreating back. But he was gone.

Chapter 20

I woke up the next morning with a head that was splitting and a mouth full of cotton. I'd had a plan before the party, which was to match each glass of wine with a glass of water, but the plan hadn't worked. Maybe I'd skipped a glass of water or something. Or it could have been the shrimp: Marvin's buffet had shrimp, and raw oysters, and raw fish wrapped in seaweed set out on boats of ice. One of the shrimp might have been bad or something.

O.K., so I had a hangover.

The telephone kept ringing. The first call, about noon, was from Erica. (Actually, Erica wasn't the first real telephone call of the day. Shortly after dawn, Olive called—how did she get my number?—something about hiring me to find a bear. I don't know what I mumbled or snarled into the phone. It could have been a dream. But I told her I'd come over to the orphanage that afternoon. I think that was what she wanted me to say anyway.)

"Hi. Is this Phyll?" Erica's voice was far too cheery for that hour of the morning.

"Hi Erica, what time is it?" I said controlling the urge to scream at her for waking me. Eric had a lovely voice, but not so early, not so early.

"Noon, a little after. Did I wake you?"

Noon. I was glad I hadn't screamed. "No. No. Just getting up for lunch."

"Oh. What a shame. We just finished breakfast. Sara and I. We'd have loved to have you over. Sara's been telling me. About what you and she talked about last night. I'm sorry I was so rude when you were here. Sara says you're really a nice person."

"Thank you."

"I thought maybe we should have you over. I mean I should. For dinner or something."

Lady, I thought, it's not that early in the morning. First Sara turns on the charm and then you. What question don't you want me to ask? Who don't you want me to talk to? "We should get together," I said.

"I thought of asking you to dinner here. But I don't know. I was so rude to you the last time. How about if we have breakfast together somewhere. On neutral ground. I'll pay."

"Breakfast?"

"That's my one big meal. I'm trying to slim down."

"How about lunch right now? I'll pay."

"Oh I'd love to, but we just ate."

"Dinner tonight then."

"I want to but I'm meeting someone. Breakfast tomorrow. It's the first open slot on my calendar. I promise you."

"Breakfast tomorrow then. I should get up earlier anyway."

"You should. We working people do."

"I thought you jocks got to sleep in every morning, go down to the park around noon and shag a few flies."

"Right. Or if we have a night game, sleep in till four, put in a few hours on the court, and party till dawn. You're thinking of those big time sports like baseball and hockey. During the week, I work nine to five like everybody else. After work, I head for the beach and get an hour or two on the sand. When it gets too dark to see, I go to the gym for an hour or two more of practice. Weekends, I throw away the starched blouse, jacket, and phony tie that make me look like I rent cars, and try again to win the big one."

"How are you doing?" I asked.

"You saw me the last time I was out."

Oops. "I'll see you tomorrow, Erica."

Marlene telephoned. Apparently, I'd been forgiven. This was a dinner invitation. She also wanted to let me know the latest

Chapter in the soap opera. Valerie had threatened suicide. Not attempted it, mind you, or succeeded, merely threatened. I wasn't impressed. I just hoped Valerie wasn't going to be a third at dinner. Marlene has a weakness for stray animals.

I telephoned JoAnne Greene; we were due for another confab. I got someone on the phone who mumbled, then I got Potzie who said, "What do you want cretin?," then I got a dial tone.

Mike Purdy called. He wanted to know if I'd put my list of clues together yet. I told him I was working on it and asked how Diane was. He said she had a headache, she'd eaten some bad shrimp at a party, but that she'd probably be O.K. by the weekend.

I had a couple of wrong numbers—one Chinese (oriental anyway), and one black, looking for a cleaners; I have my own dirty clothes pile, thank you.

I spent the afternoon on the beach with some very wonderful kids, and let the answering machine take over in my absence. The bear mystery—the pretext for Olive's call—was quickly resolved and we were able to get down to some serious socializing. Olive wanted to see a mushy movie and Todd a "dirty harry," while Greg opted inexplicably for a "Chinese opera." The beach proved to be what everyone needed.

The next to the last phone call of the day was from Derek, about 10:30 p.m. I'd just gotten back from dinner—it was dreadful thank you. Valerie was there and all she did was wail. But now Potzie was her problem. The husband called up once and she wasn't even interested. I could have told her Potzie was bad news and did and that just started her wailing again. Marlene told me to shut up. I told Marlene I'd just as soon not spend the night. It was that kind of evening.

"McSorley's saloon, we're closed for the evening." I snarled into the telephone.

"I have to talk to you," Derek said.

"Why?" I hadn't enjoyed my first meeting with Derek and had rather hoped it would be my last. Or was I just jealous of Barbara's last boy toy?

"I'm a suspect aren't I? Well, I've got some information that would interest you."

"Eleven o'clock tomorrow, my office," I snapped.

"It would be better if I saw you tonight."

"Better for who? Whom?" I corrected.

"You're saying it's too late for us to meet tonight?"

"Yes."

"Could we meet first thing in the morning, then?"

"I have a date."

We finally settled on six a.m. (yech) at the health club where I'd met him the first time. "You'll be out on the boardwalk?" I asked.

"No, inside."

"And why am I coming to see you again?" One doesn't get information if one doesn't ask questions.

"I think I know who killed Barbara."

Now he tells me. My dreams that evening, which normally feature bikini-clad blonds, were now filled with little brown men, impenetrable jungles, and automatic assault weapons. A little man would pop out of the jungle ahead of me, weapon leveled. I'd grab the gun, wrestle it away from him, and he'd disappear. Pop, yank. Pop, yank, just like an arcade game.

I woke up in a cold sweat when Derek called me again a half hour later. He said our meeting would have to be for 6:30 a.m. instead. "Too late," I said.

“It’s not me,” he said, “It’s the other person we’ll be meeting.”

Which left one more phone call that had to be made. I called Erica and told her I might be late for breakfast. She asked why and suggested that we move our meal to a restaurant near Derek’s health spa called the Landing Field, “Did I know it?” I knew it. The Landing Field’s prices are outrageous, but you get to see the chef flipping buckwheat pancakes through a plate glass window while you dine and the pancakes come with real butter and real maple syrup. Real blueberries, too, if you want them.

I had trouble getting back to sleep. There were too many unanswered questions: Why 6:30 the next morning? Who was the other person? The little brown men were waiting for me when I did drift off. They pursued me for most of the night and I was more or less grateful when the alarm woke me for my appointment with Derek.

At 6:30 a.m., the boardwalk was still in misty twilight. You could see an occasional car’s lights on the nearby street, but mostly it was gray and still. Down on the beach, a group of figures were standing in a circle. The leader would bend down to the sand, make a grunting noise, then lift his hands to the sky as if making an offering. One by one the others would imitate his movements. Weight lifters. Hard to believe that one was a future governor.

The entrance to the health spa was darker than the boardwalk had been. A motorcycle, its front fender smashed and twisted, lay asprawl the sidewalk where someone had tried to lean it against the building. On second glance, it was not the fender but the wheel itself that was bent. The cycle had obviously had an argument with an automobile and lost.

I had a vision of a dozen or so amateur athletes waiting inside the spa, scoffing down carrot juice and croissants at the health bar. But when I stepped into the foyer, the studio was deserted, doors open, and lights out. Derek, what do you have planned for me?

A shadowy figure was reflected over and over in the dozen mirrors that lined the entrance hall. Some effort had been made to style the creature's hair, but the overall effect was not promising. I wondered if Derek had a clean shirt I could borrow before I went off to meet Erica for breakfast. Men's clothes, three sizes too large, are my favorites.

The reception desk was at the end of the mirrored hallway. If memory served, the indoor track and the Nautilus room could be reached from there. Actually, there were three doorways at the end of the hall, each opening into a darkened room. I chose the darkest—why postpone the suspense—and found myself stumbling along a line of lockers. An open locker door caught me in the cheek; a moment later, a second door smashed into my knee. Hi everybody, I'm here. But I was alone with my breathing. I could hear a drip, drip, drip from the showers. Then behind me, in another part of the building, I heard a door slam, running footsteps, a second door opening, probably the one to the building, and then silence.

The shower room was a dead end. On the way back, a small amount of light from the hallway revealed the open locker doors. I only stumbled once on the bench between the rows of lockers and cracked my shin.

At the reception desk, a door that had been open was now closed. I opened it. More mirrors, reflecting little sparks of light from the windows in the hall. Benches, mats, weights and pulleys, and superimposed on top of them, my own image reflected in the doorway.

I discovered the blood on the light switch after I flipped the lights on. The mats where Derek lay were covered with the blood that seeped from the stab wounds in his chest. Someone had opened a terrible gash in Derek's abdomen and his intestines has been pushed up and out during the struggle. Someone had dragged Derek's pants down or he had been tricked into stepping part way out of them. The attacker had hacked at Derek's groin with a knife or a razor until Derek's penis had been severed completely from his body. The mutilated penis and one of Derek's testicles lay side by side on the floor. The remaining testicle, still partially attached to the scrotum, was hanging by a dangling bloody thread.

I wasn't sick. What I saw, I saw by taking a series of quick peeks at the body, stepping outside in the hallway where I would breathe slowly and deeply, and then creeping back to look again. Whoever had killed Derek had killed him slowly, clumsily, perhaps fighting with him at the end, when Derek finally had time to react. Cuts and scratches, defensive wounds covered Derek's hands and arms as well as his body.

A brown-skinned cleaner, scarf over her hair, came into the weight room dragging a vacuum cleaner. The plug to the cleaner was in her other hand. She saw the body, saw me, put the hand with the plug up to her mouth, and ran from the room. I didn't blame her. My one concern was that she would link me somehow with Derek's killing.

What kind of a person would mutilate a man like that?A homosexual, I thought, taking revenge on another homosexual, or a sicko lesbian taking her anger out on every man.

I didn't get to leave immediately. The police came and I had to explain to them about the two phone calls, the Dahl murder and the investigation, the footsteps I'd heard running away when I was in the locker room, and the cleaning woman with the vacuum. They took down my story just the way I told it; the only quarrel they had was with my description of the cleaning woman. "The cleaners come at night," they said.

The plain-clothes detectives arrived and took me through the story a second time. One of them wanted to take my p.i.

license and one of them wanted to arrest me. They called Marvin but all they got was his answering machine. Then they tossed it up to a Lieutenant. He said they could let me go, I was harmless, but they took me through my story a third time just to be sure.

I got to the Landing Field a half an hour late for my appointment with Erica. I'd hoped she would be still be there waiting for me. She wasn't. The maitre d' said there hadn't been anyone answering Erica's description at the restaurant that morning.

Chapter 21

"Who is it?" she said through the closed door.

"It's me, Phyllis Ludwigsohn." I pushed the buzzer a second and then a third time. Sara inched the door open and peeked out. "Phyllis?" she said tentatively. I stepped into the crack and pushed past her into the narrow entrance way. "Where is she?" I demanded.

It hadn't taken me long to put the case together. Derek Chzynski had figured out who the murderer was. Not surprising, considering that he had access to all of Barbara's private papers. Next, he'd called her and tried to put the squeeze on. The killer had agreed and they'd arranged to meet the next morning. Judging by the way Derek had been caught with his pants down, the payment was to be in sex. But he wasn't content with simple blackmail. He'd also arranged for me to be there a half hour after payment was made. Barbara's killer would go to jail and Derek would have the added fillip of knowing she'd been totally humiliated. A great plan, almost Sicilian in its genius. But it had all gone wrong when I phoned the murderess to let her know where I would be the next day.

"Where is she?" I asked again, "Where is Erica?"

"I'm all alone this morning," Sara said coyly. She was wearing a pink terry cloth bathrobe that softened the line of her breasts, yet emphasized how full and firm they were. The robe was cinched tight around her slim waist by a wide yellow cord; the robe flared out and up immediately to a woman's hip, then down but not a long way down her long silken legs. I finished the inspection and looked up again at Sara's face.

She was trying her best to look childlike and demure and eminently kissable. I didn't kiss her.

"Where is she?" I said.

"I can't tell you."

"Erica didn't keep her appointment with me."

"She... she had no choice. Her husband was going to move the children."

Before I could ask any more questions, the telephone rang. "I'll answer it," I said.

"This is Officer Merz with the Tolucca Hills Police department. Is Sara Newcombe there?"

"It's for you," I said and handed Sara the phone receiver.

"Yes. No. No, she hasn't come home yet. No, I don't know where she is. I understand. Yes. No, he's just a friend. Of mine. She didn't. I already told you."

Sara hung up. She looked ready to cry. She did cry; she threw her arms around me and cried like a baby. Her breasts were warm and full and my own nipples softened which I knew was the totally wrong response to the situation. There wasn't much I could do about it.

I patted Sara on the back. She wailed. I patted her on the butt, which pushed her thighs against me. I stood helpless and stroked her flanks and the curve of her hip and the swell of her breasts. She reached her head up and kissed me and I kissed her. "I'm sorry," I said. She looked at me wide-eyed. Then she kissed me. She kissed me again. I kissed her. The bathrobe cord came untied and slid down to the floor around her ankles. I kissed her breasts and then I kissed her belly. She was the most beautiful woman I had ever beheld.

We tried to make love on the couch, sinking back into the heavy pillows, fumbling and awkward. "You're trying too hard to be gentle," she said. And when I remained quiet, content to be beside her, she said, "Move. I like it best when you move."

I was moving when the phone rang. "I've got to answer the phone," she said, "I've got to." I looked at her helplessly as she pulled away. "I'll be back," she said and slipped off the couch running for the phone.

"Yes. Oh, where are you Erica? The police have been calling. They called twice. Phyll's here. Phyllis Ludwigsohn. She says she's sorry she didn't meet you (this last to me). You've got to go to your lawyer. No, do what the lawyer tells you. You'll have to give them back Erica. He's not a monster, he's a nice guy. Just call your lawyer. I'm sorry." Sara collapsed to the floor and began to cry, a thin tuneless wail that echoed the one coming through the phone.

After awhile, she hung up the receiver. When she didn't come back to the couch, I walked over to her, pulling on my clothing as I went. "Erica's all right?" I said, trying to be reassuring, not really asking a question. Sara threw her arms around me; again I tried to find someplace to put my own arms and the fumbling hands on the ends of them. I thought again of that other goddess, the one in the photograph, the sudden stabbing pain before she dropped that one last time to the sand. I thought of Derek lying in a pool of his own blood.

"Where is Erica?" I said to her roughly.

She stopped crying. She looked me full in the face, biting on her lower lip. After a moment, she turned her head away. "I can't tell you," she said.

"But you know where she is." She nodded. "You told Erica you wouldn't tell?" She nodded again. "And you lied to the police didn't you? Twice. What did Erica do?" Sara looked at me helplessly and began to cry again. The sobs contorted her face and shook her entire body.

Slowly, I turned Sara's face to mine again. "Erica kidnapped her children, didn't she?" A nod. "She took them from the private school they've been going to in the mornings. And now she doesn't know where to go with them.

"Did she steal them this morning when she was supposed to be having breakfast with me?" I grabbed Sara under the chin.

"Yes." Sara looked surprised and hurt. I had hurt her when I grabbed her. I had wanted to hurt her, I suppose. She still didn't know what I knew, that Derek Chzynski lay dead in the health spa, a dozen stab wounds in his chest and abdomen, his penis severed from his body. But not by Erica Mueller. She had her own enormous grief.

Then who killed Derek?

Chapter 22

"JoAnne Greene!" I said.

"JoAnne Greene?"

"JoAnne killed Derek."

"Killed Derek!" Again, Sara's high alto echoed my own lower tones. She had a sexy voice, a good match for her sexy body. I kissed her again. Then, I told her about Derek's murder. I left out the details of course.

"But why do you think JoAnne did it?" she asked as soon as I was through. So I had to tell her the details. Some of them.

"Poor Derek," she said, both her voice and her face expressing concern. "But why do you think it was JoAnne? A lot of us thought that, well, Derek was a perfect match for Barbara. I mean he was gay, too."

"Don't you think it would more likely be one of Derek's male friends? I mean someone he'd worked out with down at the spa? Why do you think it's one of us? I mean a woman. Isn't it more likely a man would do it? It sounds like such a horrible crime."

I hadn't told her the half of it. Partly because I didn't think she needed to know. Partly because I didn't want to think about the details myself.

"Two reasons I think it's a woman," I said. "First, Derek was going to tell me the name of Barbara's killer. Derek was the only male suspect. Ergo his murder had to be a woman, one of the others. Second, a man would never have done that to another man."

“Yes, he would,” Sara persisted, “Don’t you remember in Philadelphia when this professor burst into his lover’s apartment, shot him and the man he was in bed with, hacked off their sex organs and then threw them out the window?”

“Whoever cut off Derek’s genitals did it while he was still alive, while he was still fighting. Derek had cuts and scratches all over his face and his arms and that’s the third reason I think Derek was killed by a woman.”

“Men can have long fingernails. Women can have short ones.”

I looked at Sara’s fingernails. She looked back undismayed and matched me stare for stare. “You bite yours I see.” I said, breaking the silence.

“Only when I’m nervous.” She giggled, “Oh God, I’m so worried about Erica.”

“Will she give herself up?”

“I hope so. You thought Erica killed Derek didn’t you?”

“Yes.”

“Erica could never have done anything like that, never.” Sara said fiercely. I wondered who she was trying to convince with her fierceness. “You didn’t think it was me did you?”

“No, I didn’t think it was you. Did you kill Barbara?” I asked.

“No. You’re still not sure about me are you?”

“I’m sure and I’m not sure.”

“I could never kill anyone.” Sara said.

I mimicked Sara using her knife on the orange. “Oh that was different. Yes I could kill someone if they attacked me. But I would try not to kill them. I would try to get them to stop.”

“Maybe that’s just what this person did.” I said, “Tried to get Derek to stop and he just kept coming. He was pretty upset about Barbara. He loved her.”

“Love,” she said disparagingly.

“I love you,” I said.

“You lust after me”

“Well O.K., I do, but I’m getting to the other thing.”

“And how’s Marlene?” she said.

I looked embarrassed. I mean, I felt embarrassed and I probably looked as guilty as I felt. “Marlene didn’t seem to worry you a few moments ago,” I said. “She still doesn’t worry me,” Sara replied. She walked over and kissed me. The housecoat fell open again.

“I’ve got to find the killer,” I said coming up for air.

“Now that you’ve got what you wanted.”

“I’ve got to find the killer because that’s my job. Then I’ll come back.”

“I want to help you,” she said.

“Thanks. But it’s hard to see what you could do.”

“I’ll go see JoAnne.”

“That’s crazy.”

“No, she’ll be glad to see me. She’d like to have me back.”

“And the others. The rest of that crazy Manson family?”

“This for the girls,” she said and snapped her fingers, “Besides, they’d like to have me back too regardless of what they say. Can you imagine me and Potzie?”

I could, but my thoughts were strictly X-rated.

“Which of us do you think is more attractive?

For a moment the two images were superimposed in my mind: Potzie’s crayoled cheeks and fierce determined jaw, Sara’s own warm smile, and then Marlene’s face and somewhere in there Diane Purdy and Chara too, a warm toothy grin, a flash of slim brown leg. Many faces, one face. The differences were not in the cheekbones or the size of the bust line but in a touch on the arm, the warmth in a glance, and the way her voice changed when she realized it was me on the telephone. It really wasn’t how a person looked that mattered, it was how she felt about you, the sharing and the caring that took place between the two of you.

"Marlene said something about going to see JoAnne, or Potzie, anyway." I said, dodging the question.

"She can't handle it."

"No," I agreed. "I'm not sure I could handle it either. And I should check on that cleaning woman I saw."

"You go to the cleaners and I'll go to JoAnne's."

"How will we communicate?"

"The answering machine, silly. Most of us have an answering machine that works." She showed me how to set the machine and how to punch in the code that would rewind the tape and let you listen to as well as record a message from a remote location. It was hard to believe an answering machine could do all that, but then my own answering machine never did much of anything at all.

My first stop was the police station, not the health spa. I figured the detectives had all the details by now and might be willing to share them with me. I was wrong. I didn't get past the desk Sergeant. Two young black kids who couldn't have been more than thirteen laughed at me when the Sergeant told me to buzz off. I glared at them and they looked away. At least, I could scare somebody.

I tried phoning the police detectives from a payphone just outside the police station. I didn't get the desk Sergeant but I did get someone who wanted to know my name, address, social security number, and area code. She also wanted to know my telephone number. I gave her the one in the phone booth and she said the detectives would get back to me. Score two for their side.

It always seems so easy on T.V. The detective has a buddy who works on the police force. The buddy gets the p.i. all the information she needs. I didn't have a buddy and the only police I'd come in contact with so far had treated me like scum or at best like a member of the public, which for them might well be the same thing.

As long as I was in the phone booth, I invested another quarter and called Sara's answering machine. Sara hadn't checked in yet, neither had Erica. Officer Merz of the Tolucca police force had called, so had somebody named Deena who wanted Sara to call her. Oh well, the day was young yet.

The spa seemed to have completely recovered from the early morning's events. Guys in short sleeve shirts and long flood pants were strolling in and out with their sports bags as they had the first day I was there to see Derek. The desk was manned again and the attendant and a young friend were busy admiring themselves in the mirrors.

I asked for the manager and the attendant said that was he. I said I didn't think so and asked if I could speak to the boss instead. Pretty boy sniffed and gestured across the hallway. It took me a moment, but finally I realized that what I'd thought was just another mirror was really the door to an office. I'd missed it completely that morning. Maybe Derek had too; probably, nobody but the people who worked there knew about it.

The man who sat behind the desk had as much hair as Mike Purdy, his nose and ears were full of it; he also had about 200 more pounds on him than Mike had. I didn't like him, maybe because he didn't fit my image of the health spa.

"I already talked to you guys," he said, when I told him I wanted to ask him a few questions.

I explained that I was a private detective and not a cop. "Then I don't need to talk to you," he said. I told him I was from the insurance company and they wouldn't pay off until I completed my investigation. "O.K., I talk to you, then." A perfectly agreeable fellow.

I didn't learn much. Derek was just another paying customer, though a two-year old membership in the club entitled him to certain privileges, like a full-length locker instead of a half-length one. It was clear the owner couldn't have told Derek from any of the other muscle bound clones that patronized his establishment or cared to. Unlike the self-absorbed type at the desk in the hallway, he didn't even particularly care for men. "They not so dirty as women," he said, explaining the spa's male-only policy. He clearly wanted fast turnover, money up front, and low expenses. It's the American way.

I got the address of the cleaners from him, "but they only come in the evening," he admonished. Then I went outside to phone Sara again. The guy wouldn't let me use the phone in his office, not without a quarter anyway.

The messages from the policeman and Deena repeated themselves and then Sara came on the line: "Erica, I hope you are home now. Everything is going to be all right, honey. It will just take a little time to work things out. But things will get better. Believe me. Mr. Bridgeman says that you are going to be able to see your children, even bring them home on weekends. We're going to win, but you have to be patient.

"I'm around the corner from JoAnne's now. Phyllis asked me to visit her. By now, you must know what happened. If you don't, just ask Phyll.

"Phyllis. In case you're listening in. JoAnne wasn't there when I got there—she had a meeting or something, but most everybody else was, and they were all glad to see me, so there. Nobody was talking about you know what. I didn't say anything, just listened, but if they did know, if they had been the ones, I'm sure somebody would have said something. I was there for almost forty-five minutes talking with Potzie and Deborah. Potzie remembers you; Deborah is as vague as always.

"Oh Erica, do you remember Gail Kolodny? She's been staying here for a week. She's given up completely on the

East Coast and wants to try beach ball, of course. Wait till she finds out we have three East Coast dates on the tour this year."

Sara went on talking about Gail and a few other names I didn't recognize, but I tuned her out. One thing was clear, nobody at JoAnne's place had been involved in the attack on Derek. Or had they faked Sara out? While Sara was in the living room talking with Potzie and Deborah and Gail Kolodny, were Derek's attackers in the back of the house sleeping or trying to sleep? And who was to say that JoAnne really went to her meeting, those deceitful amazons who'd ambushed me on the volleyball court?

As if she had been reading my mind, I heard Sarah say, "Incidentally, I walked all around the house looking for clues; I didn't just stay in the living room talking with Deborah and Potzie. Everything is just normal; people are talking about who they've seen and what they're going to do. The girls are really swell. I think it's just you they didn't like. Sorry Phyll.

"Erica, the welcome mat is out for you, too. But I think we'd better just stay home tonight, just the two of us. Things will get better. I'm going back to JoAnne's in about a half an hour, that's when she's expected. Then I'm coming right home. Bye. I love you." She hung up.

I left the telephone in my ear while I digested this. The tape recorder hissed silently at the other end of the line. O.K. Sara had checked in with the Manson family, found them creepy as always, but no signs of any "extra" activity.

The tape recorder burst into life again. Apparently Sara had called back a second time. "Hi. I'm still at JoAnne's. JoAnne's home and we're all going out to CoCo's for lunch." There was the sound of giggling in the background. Sara's voice dropped a decibel as she whispered into the phone, "The meeting JoAnne was at. There was another department head, two deans, and the college president."

Her voice rose back to normal as she added, "Erica, honey, I will call you just as soon as we get back. I'll keep calling all afternoon. If you need anything or need me to go anywhere, just leave a message on the tape." There was a beep and the recorder lapsed into silence. Sara hadn't mentioned my name again and other than the brief reference to JoAnne's faculty meeting, there'd been no sign that Sara still remembered me. I hung up.

Chapter 23

Reynolds Janitorial Service, also known, according to the yellow pages, as the Sam Reynolds Janitorial Service, was located on Windsor Road no more than three blocks from the health spa. The Windsor Road address might have provided deluxe office space when it was first constructed, but that was a long time ago. Shabby was the word today. A circular desk in the vestibule that had once been a home away from home for a security guard, now held three giant canisters on wheels, overflow from the Sam Reynolds Janitorial Service, no doubt. There was an importer, an exporter, a Sam Wong D.D.S., the Reynolds Agency, Reynolds Janitorial Service, and the Sam Reynolds Janitorial Service. The latter three were all on the same floor.

One of the four elevators was currently on the 3rd floor where the various Reynolds' enterprises were located, the remainder were on the top floor of the building. As I watched the indicators, the elevator on the 3rd floor rose to the 5th floor and then dropped back again. The lights on the other elevators stayed put. Somehow, I suspected that only one of the elevators was working. Probably only one had been working since the current crop of tenants moved in. It was that kind of building.

The elevator worked, barely. It has been inspected some time in the not too distant past, though the date of inspection appeared to have been smeared with grease, deliberately I'm sure. I had plenty of time to check out the inspection certificate, even on a trip to the third floor. An elevator ride to the top floor of the building would have taken all day.

The contrast between the dim fluorescent lighting in the elevator and the sunlight streaming through the window at one end of the 3rd floor hallway meant I was completely blind for the first three or four minutes I was there. When my vision returned amid a swarm of fluttering black dots, I made out the Sam Reynolds Janitorial Service and the Reynolds Agency. Both doors were locked. And no one came to answer my knock.

The other end of the hallway was lost in the gloom. Building management didn't believe much in light bulbs. I walked slowly, letting my eyes adjust. I wondered what the tenants did at night or did they rent only to creatures that could see in the dark.

The dark end of the hallway was home to the Sam Reynolds Service Agency. A bespectacled Negro with a brown fedora was painting a name on the remaining empty door. Reynolds Enterprises, it read. Somehow, I wasn't surprised. "I'm looking for the cleaning service," I said.

"Which one you wan, black or brown?" The accent was thick, uncultured, somewhere between Tuskegee (Alabama) and Fitzgerald (Georgia). The man had thick lips, a wide loose mouth, jug ears, and huge unblinking eyes. He looked a lot like Junior Walker, the black comedian, except for the horn rim glasses. A thin pencil moustache completed the joke but he might have thought it was handsome. I wonder what he thought of me.

"Brown or black, what's the difference?" I said.

"Brown ge's you a bunch a little brown men to clean yo' office, black ge's you a bunch a fat colored ladies."

"I'm looking for brown," I said.

"O.K."

I waited for him to say more, but he'd gone back to examining his sloppy lettering with all the intensity of an impressionist gazing at the Seine. "Well?" I said, in my best Jack Benny voice.

"Yes?"

"Which office is the brown?"

"They ain't in."

"Where ..." I began.

"They's out to lunch."

"The black then!"

"Same thing. Of course," he went on when he saw I was an inch from reaching for my nonexistent gun, "You could try downtown, at the head office."

"What's the number!"

"They gots it inside." He jerked his finger toward the closed door. "Of course," he said again, as he watched my face go through much the same color changes as a lobster put to boil—white folks can be a lot of fun sometimes, "Mista Reynolds, could be in the field."

"Who the hell are you?" I said.

"Sam Reynolds, A.B., M.B.A.," he said with a considerably uptown accent.

"I see. And where's the A.B. from?"

"Harvard," he said in cultured tones and an accent that was pure Bostonian. "Philosophy. Would you like to Hegel a little?"

"Philosophy? Not much opportunity for a degree in philosophy." I said thoughtfully, as if I'd actually completed an intended degree in criminal justice at Pasadena City College.

"Not much opportunity for a black boy with a degree in anything. But you're right, philosophy don't cut it. That's why the M.B.A."

"Is that from Harvard, too?" I asked respectfully.

"No, that's from a mail-order house in Kansas City. But it done me about as much good as the degree in philosophy. They already had a black boy in the firms I applied to."

"One."

"One's all they need."

"So you went into the service business," I said to fill the conversational gap.

"Three offices—the one you see, one downtown, and one in Tolucca City. And over 100 employees, course they don't all show up for work."

"I'm impressed," I said.

"I'm philosophical about it."

"Do you think you could find me the address of one particular employee?"

"I could try." He took a heavy key ring out of his pocket and waved it back and forth across the hallway. "What's the name?"

"I don't know."

He regarded me with considerable amusement. I could understand why. "What company she work for?" he asked indulgently. I gave him the name of the health spa. "The downtown branch?"

"No, right here in Santa Monica."

"That'd be black, then."

"No brown. She'd be brown. I mean Hispanic."

"Hmm. And how'd you meet this groovy chick?"

I told him, leaving out the bits about the deserted hallway and the pool of blood on the weight room floor. "Not mine," he said, "We cleans evenings."

"That's what they told me."

"Who did?"

"Ahm. Oh never mind. Thanks."

"Don't mention it."

We stared at each other. Clearly, he enjoyed my company—I make a great straight man—and I was getting to enjoy his. But where could we take it from here? For that matter, where could I take this investigation? There were no more clues, no more suspects. "Look, do you own this company?" I asked on a hunch.

"I might."

"All of it?"

"Not all of it."

"Could you tell me who also owns part of the company?" I asked.

"Like who?"

"Like JoAnne Greene?"

"Nope."

"Diane and Mike Purdy?"

"Nope."

"I could go downtown and search the records, you know."

"I ain't shucking you, white bread. Go downtown if you like, but you wasting yo time." His country accent had come back in full. "Are these people brothers?" he asked.

"Brothers?"

"Soul brothers. This is a 100% minority-owned business."

"Dee-Dee Williams," I said.

Chapter 24

She answered the telephone on the first ring, as if she had been waiting all that afternoon, every afternoon since the murder for me to call. When she wasn't following me around in her silver-gray limousine, of course.

"You want me to come to your office. I'll come to your office. This evening, after dark." The voice was cold, lifeless. Not at all the way I remembered it.

That left me with a long afternoon to kill, typing up the facts, making a presentation for Marvin. Telling him I was sorry the investigation had taken so long. Telling him to send the check he owed me as a donation to Barbara's Kids. And, oh, had he given any thought to renaming them "Erica's Kids."

I went into Penny's to buy some socks and a pair of pants, and, would you believe it, there were almost no other customers, no lines at the fitting rooms or the cash register. I was in and out in ten minutes. The "five pictures for $3.50 (three bucks for senior citizens) cinema" next door offered an assortment of golden oldies, plus two recent B pictures, but I wasn't that anxious or depressed, I just wanted a way to get through the afternoon.

It was a quiet day on the beach. It's not that far from my office and I walked there. I didn't think that anybody would be following me and they weren't. I hoped Chara would be there and she wasn't. But I ran for half an hour and got some of the excess adrenalin out of my system.

It was a good thing I got back to my office half an hour before my appointment with the murderess. That half hour gave me a chance to let my eyes grow accustomed to the dark. Dusk had changed to night outside my window. The surf was a far off whisper. The only illumination in the room came from the gooseneck lamp on my desk, carefully pointed toward the visitor's chair.

In the shaded area of the hallway where she crouched, half in and half out of my office, she was all but invisible. She could have been holding a gun aimed at me, but I didn't think so, it was not my Black Madonna's style. Poisons were her style, and formula, and lots of bottles.

A Madonna without child this time, I saw.

"Barbara Dahl was a bitch, a dirty racist bitch," Dee-Dee said.

"That's not enough to kill for."

"Not enough for you gray meat, but it was enough for me. You never growed up where people called you nigger. You didn't have to put up with 'nigger bitch' each time you came onto the court, or watch your proud mama sit alone at each one of your games, while the other girls' parents, the white girls' parents, their mothers and fathers all sat clustered together.

"If once, just once, one of them would have said, 'Ms Williams, you come sit with us,' but none of them ever did.

"I'm proud I'm black, you know."

"I know there are times I'm not proud I'm white."

"That Barbara. You know I don't play beach ball, but there's lots of girls that would like to, Roberta and Keesha. She fixed it so they couldn't."

"That's impossible."

"You think so, white lady. Think anybody can play. You try to sign up sometime when you're black. You're always a little too late, a little too black.

"But Barbara, Barbara had the power. She had the endorsements and what she said went; everybody knew that.

And Barbara was Klan; you know that. Barbara, Sara, they're all racists."

"But one crazy family, doesn't mean . . ."

"They had the power. I look down at my little boy and I say to him, you not going to grow up in that kind of world."

"So you fixed the water bottle."

"So I put the poison in her water bottle. How'd you know?"

"It had to be you. You were the only one at courtside who was busy mixing formula and swapping bottles all afternoon. Didn't you worry about giving the wrong bottle to your baby by mistake?"

She had to think about that one. I guess she hadn't thought it all through. Enough maybe to take out plenty of insurance. But not enough to think that a kid who grows up with both a mother and a father may be better off than a kid with lots of money that has only one.

"I'm going now." she said. "You can tell my son what I did and why I did it. Later, when he grows up. You're not going to stop me are you, Ms. Ludwigsohn?"

I recognized the gun she was holding. It was my gun, the one I'd bought on an impulse, five or six years before when some mug threatened my life. After he got sent up, I'd stashed the gun in my office drawer, and never looked at it again. Until now.

"No. I'm not going to try to stop you."

The greatest woman volleyball player in the world smiled. She undid the clasp of the green felt bag she had slung over her shoulder and put the '38 inside. In one way, she was right to take me at my word. I wasn't going to be a hero, wrestle for the gun, and take her into custody. But mentally, I was taking the cover off the old manual typewriter and starting to hunt and peck a final addition to my report to Marvin, "My esteemed Sir, the murderess you seek is none other than ..."

"Good-bye White lady."

She slipped into the shadows. There were the unexpected sounds of a scuffle just outside my office door; I heard rather than saw the blows. Then I saw Dee-Dee Williams fall heavily to the ground. A second dark-skinned figure slipped Ninja-like into the light, the cleaner from the spa, my old flame from the beach. She smiled, a gleaming toothy smile as she easily threw Dee-Dee's prostrate form across her shoulders. I recognized the still-remembered, well-loved aroma of her feminine perfume. "Chiao," she said with a flash of gleaming teeth, and then both she and her burden vanished again into the darkness.

Dee-Dee Williams body washed up on the shore the next day. Accidental death by drowning. A midnight swim on an unlit beach. A heavy undertow. The city of Long Beach is not responsible for accidents after dark when lifeguards are no longer on duty.

I told Melvin the whole story, of course. Well, almost the whole story. I told it the way I had it planned out in my mind before Dee-Dee left my office. Like Mel says, that's why you hire a private detective, so that the whole world doesn't have to know your business.

So Barbara Dahl is still a symbol of beach volleyball, bigger in death than in life. They have a memorial tournament every year, sponsored by Lackland Beer. The proceeds all go to Pro Kids, a halfway house for orphans. Dee-Dee Williams, of course, is still the greatest woman player volleyball ever had. She broke every record the game ever had. And if she hadn't died a tragic accidental death early in her career, she'd be breaking records still.

Erica Mueller and Sara Newcombe won the next big beach tournament. Diane Purdy and her partner placed third. Chara deCastro went back to Guatemala or Cuba, whichever she came from. I never did get the rumors straight.

www.ingramcontent.com/pod-product-compliance
Lightning Source LLC
LaVergne TN
LVHW051003080826
845145LV00009B/2428

* 9 7 8 0 9 8 4 1 6 0 3 1 0 *